PRAISE FOR
MY MOTHER'S BOYFRIENDS

"Witty and utterly enchanting."
—Vendela Vida, author of *We Run the Tides*

"In *My Mother's Boyfriends*, Samantha Schoech writes with precision, grace, and considerable wit on subjects ranging from the magical to the mundane. Packed with sharply observed characters and surprising sentences that masterfully turn a story inside out, this collection is as unsettling as The Big One, but so much more fun. These are voices you'll hear in your head long after you've closed the book. A terrific read with a big San Francisco heart."
—Michelle Richmond, bestselling author of *The Marriage Pact* and *The Wonder Test*

"*My Mother's Boyfriends* will both break your heart and make you smile. A dazzling set of short stories that touch on the most human of experiences; growing up, raising children, watching ailing parents, and aging. Each story is a gem full of warmth, insight, and a touch of humor. "
—Courtney Flynn, Trident Booksellers and Cafe

"Samantha Schoech's writing is a symphony of vivid imagery, powerful scenarios, and, just when you need it most, humor. *My Mother's Boyfriend* offers a thoughtful and engaging collection of stories that skillfully capture the often messy nature of familial love and how it sculpts us into who we are. It's a book that stirs empathy in anyone who has ever found themselves entangled in the web of affection and frustration within their family, inviting readers to embrace the complexity of these relationships with reflection and even grace. This book is a powerful reminder of why we call family members loved ones, making it one of the most original collections I have ever read."
—Calvin Crosby, King's English Bookshop

"I inhaled these stories! They have a feral Gen-X vibe that resonated for me, but the keen observation and humor have universal appeal."
—**Christie Olson Day, Gallery Bookshop**

"This collection of stories is a winner. I'm not a short story reader—unless they are really, really good—and I think this book nailed it. Why aren't I reading these in the *New Yorker*?"
—**Jude Sales, Reader's Books**

MY MOTHER'S BOYFRIENDS

by

Samantha Schoech

7.13 Books

Printed in the United States of America

First Edition
1 2 3 4 5 6 7 8 9

"This Is Living" appeared in the *Gettysburg Review*.
"Sudden Fictions" appeared in *ZYZZYVA*.
"The Good People of Lake George" appeared in *You Are Not Here and Other Works of Buddhist Fiction* (Wisdom Publications).
"The Phlebotomist's Boyfriend" appeared in *Seventeen*.
"Ascension" appeared in *Glimmer Train*.
"Piece of String Too Short to Use" appeared in *Kalliope*.
"Dances" appeared in *The Sun*.

Cover art by Laura Catherine Brown
Edited by Leland Cheuk

Library of Congress Cataloging-in-Publication Data

ISBN (paperback): 979-8-9877471-8-6
ISBN (eBook): 979-8-9877471-9-3

For Pete, Oliver, and Magnolia

CONTENTS

ASCENSION

I'VE JUST STOPPED BY to change clothes when I first see her wings. She's sitting there at our kitchen table with her hands wrapped around the #1 Mom mug I gave her for Mother's Day in seventh grade. At first, I run past her, but then I stop and walk backward to the open kitchen door and stare at her. Her eyes are sort of half closed in this beatific way, and there are two smooth, white humps behind her shoulders. I know she's heard me come in, but she doesn't look up; she just stays in that pose until I say, "What's up with the wings?"

She opens her eyes slowly and it takes her a moment to focus on me. When she does, her lips bend into a smile. "They're angel wings."

I roll my eyes, but I'm intrigued. My mother is not a great kidder. She's the type to light incense and candles and consult tarot cards and rune stones, but she's not the type to joke about angels.

I walk around behind her and check out the wings. She doesn't move. From the two arches above her shoulders, the folded wings descend to about her knees. They are pleated neatly and hang down over the back of her chair, folded and tucked, and huge. I touch one, and it quivers like the hide of a horse. I snap my hand back in horror.

"They're sensitive, like breasts," my mother says. She says stuff like this. She loves words like *breasts* and *vulva* and *uterus*.

"Look," she says. There's a rustling, like someone snapping a sheet before folding it, and then her wings spread out from her horizontally. She's got over a six-foot span; it's an impressive thing to witness.

They're not exactly how I've imagined angel wings to be. They have no feathers, just a thin, pearlescent membrane connecting the fine, fingerlike bones. They look like white silk bat wings, and I wonder again if she's joking, if she's rigged these elaborate wings out of fabric and pulleys, which she's manipulating beneath her poncho. But of course she isn't. These are her wings, attached with the certainty of limbs to her shoulder blades.

I walk around the table and sit across from her. She looks at me with that same calm smile, the one she has been working on since my dad left and she turned to goddess worship and transcendental meditation. It's an overcompensation thing, that smile, and usually it doesn't fool me. But now, I must admit, she looks convincingly calm. The line between her eyebrows has relaxed and her eyes are heavy-lidded.

"So what happened?" I'm aware that Claudette is waiting for me at her house. We're going to her parents' club to go swimming later, and I only just rode my bike home to get my bathing suit and a clean pair of shorts. I should be hurrying; we're trying to time our arrival with Steve Menendez's lunch break, and, by stopping to talk to my mom, I'm messing up our schedule. But my mom has grown angel wings, so I make the decision to be late.

"I woke up with them," she says, sipping from the #1 Mom mug. "My back felt a little itchy last night before I went to sleep—I was rubbing it against the door jamb, like a cow." She laughs at herself. "Then, this morning ..." She shrugs. The rest is history.

"Did anyone talk to you about them? Like, did they come with a message or anything?" My mom shakes her head and shrugs again. She hasn't a care in the world. "Well, how do you know they're angel wings if no one has, like, given you any instructions or anything?"

She looks at me with a kind of pity, and I know she's right. They are so obviously angel wings. They couldn't be anything else.

"So, you're an angel now?" It bugs me to ask this. If there's anyone on the planet who thinks she's an angel, it's my mother. It annoys me that this image of herself seems to have been realized. She nods with confidence and slowly folds her wings back down and stands up. "Are you hungry?" she asks. "I could make tomato soup and grilled cheese."

I've barely eaten at home all summer. I spend most of my time with Claudette. At her house, there are seldom parents, and the pantries are stocked with chips and sodas and cookies that the housekeeper bakes every other day. At my house, the kitchen smells of yeast and tea leaves and mildewing fruit. My mother bakes her own bread, and so any attempt at making a sandwich is thwarted by odd, uneven slices that fall apart too easily. Tomato soup is the one prepared food my mother still buys. She loves Campbell's, and although she has to make a special trip to the regular grocery store to buy it, she always has a few cans ready. I say okay and watch as she goes about the business of making lunch. Her wings bounce and shimmy slightly with her movements. The wind chimes outside tinkle and sing.

I look down at my arm, the fine hairs bleached white by the summer sun. "I thought angels had to be dead first."

"I guess not," my mother says without turning around. "Unless I died in my sleep." She laughs, but a wave of nausea passes through me. Then I look at her, turning the can opener against the soup can, and realize that even if she did die, it doesn't seem to matter. I mean, here she is. I'm looking right at her.

I stare at the place on her back where the wings are coming from. Her clothes must have slits cut in them or something, because they seem to fit all right; nothing's bunching up or anything.

"Did you cut your poncho?" I ask.

"No. It just sort of works when I get dressed. I put on my regular clothes and they just fit, and my wings are on the outside, and I don't have to struggle at all." She shakes the soup out into the pot and it lands with a splat, holding its cylindrical shape for a moment before dissolving. "Take a look," she says, coming toward me. "Tell me what's going on back there."

I stand and sort of peer around the edge of her wings, trying to see where they connect, but it seems like they disappear into the nubby wool of her poncho. I don't really want to touch them, but I'm curious. I pull the edge of the fabric away and hold open the hole so I can see the skin of her back where the wings are attached.

"It looks like a chicken," I tell her, and it does.

"Does it look irritated?"

"No." I let go of her poncho and lean against the counter.

She goes back to the stove to stir the soup and I butter the bread for the grilled cheese.

When my phone rings, my mother and I look at each other. It's as if we realize simultaneously that other people are going to find out. Word of my mother's ascension is going to get out sooner or later. I pick up. It's Claudette. "Where are you?" she pleads into the phone. "We're already totally late."

"Go without me," I tell her. "I'm gonna stay home." She exhales dramatically into the phone. She's been my best friend since the first week of middle school, but she can really be a brat. My mother says she has an over-developed sense of entitlement.

"Claudette?" my mom asks when I hang up. I nod.

"You didn't tell her."

I shake my head and continue preparing the bread.

"Do you have any, like, powers or anything?" I ask after a moment.

My mom shrugs and her wings sway slightly. "I don't know. I feel great though."

This shrugging, easygoing person is not the version of my mother I'm used to. The mother I'm used to is tense and likes lots of quiet and soft lighting. The mother I'm used to shrieks in the background when my father calls to talk to me, and then practices her breathing exercises on the living room couch until she feels centered.

"Maybe after lunch we can try some stuff."

"Like what?" my mom asks.

"Like, to see if you have any special powers."

"What kind of powers do you think I might have?" She's turned to face me again and looks excited, a little flushed.

I don't know very much about angels. I try to think of what her special powers might be, but I keep coming up with the kinds of things superheroes have, like x-ray vision and Superman hearing. Then it hits me, and I'm excited now too.

"Do you think you can fly?"

My mother grimaces and shakes her head. "I sort of tried," she says, pointing to a bruise on her forehead that I hadn't noticed. "I jumped off the landing, but I just fell and hit the bookshelf."

"Oh," I say. "That's too bad." We're silent for a moment, coming up with other tests. "Okay, what am I thinking?" I look straight into my mother's eyes, and she looks straight back into mine, frowning and unblinking. We're both concentrating very hard. This is a trick I've tried with my friends at various times over the years. Once, in sixth grade, I kept telling Rachel Grimes she was right every time she guessed what I was thinking even though what I was really thinking the whole time was how dumb she was for believing me. She still brings it up sometimes, even though we haven't been friends since junior high. She thinks we share a secret about her psychic abilities.

"Um," my mother says, "are you thinking about Taffy?"

I wrinkle my nose. Taffy was our neighbor's pony when we lived in the country when I was a little girl. I think for a minute about telling her she's right, but then I shake my head. I haven't thought about Taffy in about five years.

"So, I guess mental telepathy isn't one of them," I say.

"I guess not," my mom says, turning off the flame under the

soup and sliding the sandwiches into a heated pan. She always does this—leaves the soup in the pot for too long. It grows a skin, which I refuse to eat.

I accidentally knock over the salt shaker and then trace designs in the spilled grains with my fingers. "What about good deeds? I think angels are supposed to do good deeds. I mean, like, you're put on Earth for a reason."

My mother nods solemnly. I can tell she likes this. She's into higher purpose stuff, giving of oneself. Last summer she started volunteering at juvenile hall, but she didn't last long. Nobody signed up for her "self-esteem through beading" workshop, and I think she was really disappointed.

She puts the first grilled cheese onto a small plate and cuts it diagonally. She won't serve me until everything is ready and we can eat together. Ritual is important to her.

"Well, like, do you feel any special calling?" I ask. I'm making a series of wavy lines in the spilled salt. She looks up and drums her nails against the countertop. They are perfect, as always. Even after my dad left and my mother started dressing only in the colors of the sunset and decorating our house with batik prints of gods we can't name, she kept her weekly nail appointments. She's always been extremely well groomed.

"Um," she says again, rolling her eyes back into her skull to think. "I definitely want to do something with women." She reminds me of the way my friends and I talk when we talk about the future, except a lot of them want to be models or do something in fashion.

"Like what?"

"I don't know exactly." She looks at me with her head cocked. She's waiting for me to come up with something, but I'm not into all her goddess stuff. I shrug and pour myself a glass of milk.

"I wonder if there are certain individuals I'm supposed to look after, you know, like a guardian angel, or if I'm just here for a sense of general well-being?" she says dreamily to no one in particular.

She serves lunch, and we sit at the table facing one another. Except for the humps of her wings, she looks exactly like she always looks: smooth blondish gray hair, blow-dried with a slight flip at the ends, dangly moonstone earrings, expensive peach-colored T-shirt under her Ecuadorian poncho with llamas along the border, a skim of pink frost on her lips.

I study her for a moment while she calmly spoons tomato soup into her mouth, blowing on each spoonful beforehand, even though it's barely hot anymore. There is something different about her, but I can't place it. Occasionally she looks up at me and smiles, and then turns back to her soup. It not just the wings; it's something else.

My dad has been gone for sixteen months. He lives in Dana Point now and tells me he bought a sailboat. I've never been to visit him, although he's invited me, saying he'll pay for my plane ticket. When he calls, I don't tell my mom it was him. I can't stand how she gets when the subject of him comes up, and I can't help feeling, when I watch her face harden and her lips pinch, that I can sort of understand why my dad doesn't love her anymore. But then I feel bad because, as she's always reminding me, she gave up twenty years of her life for that man.

My mother has been pissed off since the day my father left. Big time. But now, as I look at her, and as she looks back at me with her watery, navy-blue eyes, she doesn't seem quite as mad as usual.

"Why do you think they picked you?"

"Who?" she says, as if she's lost the thread of the conversation, as if there could be anything to talk about except how she's now a heavenly being or whatever.

"I don't know. God or St. Peter or whoever. I mean, I guess we have to believe in God and everything now."

She looks up from her soup and puts down her spoon.

"I've always believed in God, just not necessarily the Christian version of one."

This is not technically true. My grandparents are Episcopalians, and I happen to know my mom spent much of her life believing in the Christian version of God. This is typical of her though; she revises freely and unselfconsciously.

"Okay," I say. "Why do you think God picked you?"

She looks back into her skull again, the little line of a smile appearing on her lips like she's remembering something pleasant.

"Well, I've been a good person."

I think of the way my mother violently sliced my father out of every single photograph in our home, the way she screamed as she tore apart their wedding album and threw its pages into the fireplace, of the way she once hissed at me, "You will have nothing to do with that bastard. He hates us and we hate him back." It's difficult for me to see my mother as an angel, but obviously she's risen to the top in somebody's estimation.

We finish our lunch, and I clean up the kitchen, and then we sit around as if we're waiting for something, only we don't exactly know what we're waiting for.

I haven't spent a single afternoon in our house all summer. There's nothing to do, really. I take a basket of my dirty laundry down to the basement and do a load. I get out the as-of-yet-unopened SAT study book I demanded my mother buy me at the beginning of summer and flip lazily through the practice tests.

My mother sits at the kitchen table with another cup of tea and works on the beaded earrings she makes and sells at the farmers' market. They're totally hippie and eighties, but she doesn't know this. She gives me a pair for every occasion. Sometimes I wear them around the house on Christmas morning to make her happy, but that's all. After Christmas, they lie in my jewelry box like sparkling, out-of-style reminders of how little my mother knows about me.

At four, Claudette calls. She's back from the club.

"I rode by your house on my way home, but I didn't stop. There was this totally weird guy standing in your front yard."

I lean over and look out the living room window, and sure enough, there's a man standing on our flagstone path looking at our house and then at a little notebook he's writing in. It looks like he's sketching, but our house looks pretty much like every other house in the neighborhood—fake Tudor, sloping front yard, little black lamppost sticking out of the lawn—so I don't know why he would do this.

"Gross," I say. "He's still there."

"Who is he? I didn't want to have to talk to him, so I just rode by." This is so Claudette. She is interested in very few people.

"I'll call you back." I hang up before she has a chance to respond. I watch the man some more. He's old, like fifty, and he's dressed in a pale-yellow golf shirt and neatly pressed khakis. He has white hair combed over to the side and dark blue boat shoes. He reminds me a little bit of my father. He continues to scribble in his book.

"Mom," I whisper, going into the kitchen where her hands are struggling with the tiny beading loom. "There's a man in the front yard."

She looks up at me slowly and her wings rise and fall like a shrug. "What do you mean?"

"Look out the window," I tell her. "Do you know that guy?"

My mother sighs and disentangles herself from the loom. Little beads skitter across the hardwood when she stands. She looks out the window for a moment, and then something occurs to her and she charges toward the front door. Her wings rustle as she passes, and I catch a smell like a burned-out match.

She rips open the front door so hard it bangs against the wall and leaves a mark, then she storms down the flagstone path toward the man in the golf shirt. He sees her and starts to back away down the path, staring like he's seen a ghost.

"He will not get this motherfucking house!" she screams. She's still coming at him, but the man is frozen in place. "It's mine, motherfucker, and he will never get it. Never."

Her performance is so dramatic, I almost start giggling. But I don't, because it's obvious she's dead serious. Instead, I stand back on the lawn and watch her. A car drives by and slows, and I see the driver crane his head and stare. It's about six o'clock, and people with regular jobs are starting to repopulate the neighborhood. My mother has stopped her advance, but she stands her ground, her chest heaving, her eyes blazing.

He gapes like he's the first person on earth ever to see a middle-aged angel in an Ecuadorian poncho, and then he makes a little sound, like a grunt, and runs back to his beige American car parked against the sidewalk. He doesn't peel out. Instead, he pulls slowly away from the curb, watching my mother until it is unsafe to do so.

When he's gone, she heads back inside. When she passes me, she stops and turns around so I almost bang into her back, into her wings. "Your father is a horrible person," she says, "and I will be damned if I'm going to let him ruin my life." She goes back into the house, but I stand outside for a while watching a dragonfly flit around the hydrangea. I want to yell back at her, to tell her that nobody likes her when she's like this, but at the moment, I'm a little afraid.

When I go back into the house, my mother is on the phone with Christof, her guide. I eavesdrop on the conversation while I make dinner: organic pasta with olive oil and parmesan and little cherry tomatoes from my mother's garden. At one point I hear her say, "Okay, I'm breathing, I'm breathing."

When she gets off the phone, I ask her if she wants dinner, but she shakes her head and goes into the living room where she puts on Tibetan chants and lights some incense. I eat alone at the kitchen table listening to the guttural intonations of the Tibetans.

By nine o'clock, my mother's fully recovered, and we watch an old episode of *Mad Men*. She has to sit in the straight-back chair so her wings can drape over and hang down the back. We pass a bowl of popcorn back and forth and drink herbal iced tea. She lets out a little cough and says, "I can't believe how they treat the women on this show." I don't say anything because, I mean, obviously. That's kind of the entire point.

When the show is over, we go upstairs to bed. I haven't been to bed this early in a long time. I wonder what Claudette is doing, and only then remember that I was supposed to call her back. I fall asleep imagining her reaction when I tell her my mom is an angel.

The next morning, I run into my mom in the hall outside our bedrooms. She's fresh from the shower, wrapped in a thick white towel, and she looks beautiful. Her wings are still there, hanging down her back and sparkling with little droplets of water.

"Beautiful day," she says, grinning. I squint at her and then head into the bathroom to pee.

When I go downstairs, my mother has made us oatmeal for breakfast, and she's cooked the raisins in, which is the way my dad and I like it.

"Is it uncomfortable to sleep?" I ask as I pour syrup into my oatmeal.

"I don't think I've slept so well in years." She takes a deep laundry-detergent-commercial breath, stretches her arms, and says, "I feel absolutely glorious."

I get up for the milk, and that's when I notice the guy from the day before parked outside our house again. He's in the same yellow golf shirt. I decide not to say anything. Even though her new angel mood is a little annoying, it's way better than her shrieking.

After breakfast, I leave for Claudette's. Her parents are skiing in Chile, where it's winter, and it's the housekeeper's day off, so we'll have the place all to ourselves. Claudette's dad is a chemist, and he invented some sort of sealant, and now they're the richest family I know. I like being around them. They never yell at her about the price of clothes or cancel HBO because it's too expensive. Ever since my dad left, my mom has been on what she calls her belt-tightening campaign. She earns a little money from her beading, but mostly we live off child support.

I decide to see what the guy in the golf shirt is up to. As I approach his car, he starts to fumble with the keys as if he's afraid of me, but when I tap on the window, he rolls it down and smiles tightly.

"Why are you in front of our house?"

"Are you Patricia?" he asks, raising his eyebrows expectantly, as if it would be a great relief if I were.

"No. That's my mom. And everyone calls her Patty."

"Is she home?"

"Yeah. Why?"

He glances at a clipboard lying next to him on the seat, and then shrugs and rolls up the window again without answering.

"Whatever," I say, hopping on my bike. My mom's going to kill him if he tries to fuck with her about the house.

At Claudette's, we watch movies in their entertainment room and give ourselves pedicures. I paint my toes red, white, and blue for the Fourth of July. Claudette does hers in Pussycat Pink. Later, when our toes are dry, we'll walk to the club to swim. I don't mention my mom's wings. She's already considered a little strange.

It's late when I get home from Claudette's and the house is dark. I put my bike in the garage and go in through the kitchen. I'm on my way upstairs when I notice a lump on our couch covered in a purple chenille throw blanket. I tiptoe back across the living room. It's the man in the golf shirt, and he's sleeping soundly, emitting a little whistle as he breathes. He's dressed in a huge white T-shirt and a pair of my sweatpants that say "Central Wildcats" in a little circle near the hip. In his sleep he looks older than he did before. He's on his side and his belly hangs, sitting solidly beside him on the couch. The sides of his eyes are crinkled like the fans we used to make out of construction paper in grade school. "La-ti-da," we would say, fluttering them in front of our faces.

I watch him for a few minutes, listening to the tick of our kitchen clock, and notice the way his mouth twitches into a smile and then relaxes, as if he is laughing in his dream.

In my bedroom the clock glows one o'clock, casting a circle of green light near my pillow. I undress and slide into bed, without even brushing my teeth. I can smell chlorine in my hair and Banana Boat on my skin. I stare through the darkness at the pimply texture of my ceiling until my eyes sting. Then I close them and fall asleep.

I awaken to a hum, some sort of low, continuous vibration. It's still dark outside when I open my eyes, but there's a weird, silvery glow in my room. I blink and prop myself up on my elbow, and only then do I notice my mother standing at the foot of my bed in her white cotton nightgown. The glow is coming from her, like a halo.

"What?" I say, sitting up.

"I found out," she says, her voice husky.

"What?" I ask again.

"They sent a messenger, like you said." When she says "messenger," she jerks her head toward the staircase, and I assume she means the golf-shirt guy.

I sit up and squint at her through my heavy eyes. "And?"

She smiles and clears her throat like she's about to audition, and then she unfurls her wings, all six feet of them, and says in a clear, loud voice, "I am the Angel of Bitterness."

I frown. "Meaning what?"

My mother rolls her eyes. She can't believe I'm not more impressed. "Meaning that's my calling."

"You go around making people bitter?"

"No!" she says, folding her wings back down against her back.

"What then?"

"I'm not exactly sure yet. He was tired." She does the head jerk toward the messenger guy again.

"But he said you were the Angel of Bitterness?"

She nods. "I think I'm like a patron saint. I'm in charge of relieving the bitter ones."

Now it's my turn to nod. I can picture this.

"So?" she says. She wants my reaction.

"So, it sounds good. I'm sure you'll be great at it." I yawn.

She sighs and her shoulders relax. "I think so, too." She smiles. "I really think I've found my calling." She stands there nodding like she's waiting for something. When I don't say anything, she says, "So ...?" again, but slowly, like there's something obvious I should be doing.

"What?"

"Well, is there anything you want to get off your chest? You know, try me out."

"You want me to confess or something?" I ask.

"Not confess, just share. Only if there's something bothering you."

I think about what I might tell her. I think about my father and his new boat and about Claudette and her rich parents. I think about the way my mother is always home bent over her beading or sitting silently, looking at nothing. I look up at her. Her wings are quivering, and her face is flushed and lovelier than I've ever seen it. But there is nothing I want to tell her. It appears her powers do not work on me.

THIS IS LIVING

ALTHOUGH IT WAS SOMETHING she disapproved of, Laurel found herself, at the ripening age of twenty-nine—okay, she knew it wasn't old, but still, the wiry gray hairs, the stretching skin of her breasts—sleeping with a married man. And what she discovered, quickly and with pleasure, was that it was only terrible in theory. In practice it was delicious, thick with a thousand forbidden things she wasn't otherwise allowed to feel. Adultery was a fabulous secret, a bitter but powerful cocktail for the blahs that came bubbling to the surface like a spring.

Even the waiting. The pitiful, clichéd waiting—and she discovered affairs were ripe with clichés—was charged with, if not exactly what she expected from her life, at least something that mimicked it. Something with drama and tragedy. A life she looked at, like she could look to a movie or play. One in which she was, at different times, both villain and heroine.

Which is why the letters were strange. Laurel had begun to write letters to his wife. At first just to sort out her feelings. She would never send them, but it gave her the chance to tell her, The Wife—Sloane—about her husband, to let her know what John was really like, what kind of lover he was when he wasn't with her, what he said in his sleep, how she made him laugh with her "oldest belly dancer in the world" routine, which she did naked and only after a few glasses of wine.

And then she did send them. Not to be cruel, although she was aware it was cruel, but because the accumulation of letters began to feel like a conversation. Sloane became the person she could talk to about her affair with John. The letters were chatty and matter of fact. There were no apologies or explanations, just a thick stack of good cream paper that formed something like a friendship.

The first letter said:

Hello Sloane,

I am the woman with whom your husband is having an affair. I assume you know something about it. In a movie, you would know. Although, it's true, I don't call the house or leave lipstick on his collar. I'm not the lipstick type. I'm not the affair type either. Or (ha!) I guess I am.

I just want you to know that this is an affair and really has very little to do with you. Still, it means you and I have quite a bit in common. I ask him about you and he is never unkind. I know you have red hair that is starting to turn gray at the temples. You never wanted children. You hate cut flowers because they remind you of funerals. You drink a bit too much red wine but are always charming when you're drunk.

She sent it on a Thursday before she and John were to spend a weekend together in wine country. Sloane thought John was on a business trip. Laurel felt a little guilty when he showed up at her apartment with his white teeth and expensive sweater and sat on her one good piece of furniture, the antique sofa she had reupholstered with velvet, while she finished packing her things: toothbrush, diaphragm, running shoes, novel.

As he drove them to Napa Valley with its easy California wealth and golden hillsides, where the restaurants were intimate and well-lit, John told Laurel she had a Jewish ass. Meaning, she supposed, that it was round and soft, that it wasn't the tame little ass she thought Sloane probably had. Laurel imagined Sloane as the color white. She saw her eating white bread and wearing white cotton underpants and driving around in a white Volvo. When she cooked, she made clean, tasteless food that never stuck in her teeth or caused bad breath. She didn't make scenes or laugh too loudly or do unattractive things absentmindedly.

Early in their affair, right when they began to feel comfortable with each other, he had made her promise. "I love you," he said, earnestly, "but I have another life. Promise me you won't make me mix them. What we have is too special—we need to keep it separate, precious." She'd swooned with ecstasy, holding his head between her hands, and whispering her promise to his lips. And until this moment she had kept her word, believing with the whole of her heart that it was sacredness that made him want to keep it secret. But she knew now, as she pictured Sloane slitting open the envelope that it was fear: shaky, tail-between-the-legs, there-are-no-atheists-in-the-trenches fear.

In Napa, they strolled around St. Helena holding hands, walking aimlessly through antique shops and stores with hundreds of varieties of mustard. He wore expensive jeans and comfortable brown shoes. His black hair curled around his ears. When she found a piece of furniture she liked, he would say in a too-loud voice, "So honey, do you want it for the den or the bedroom?" He thought he was very funny. And Laurel played along although she was quite aware that he, unlike her, lived in a house with a den—one furnished with expensive modular furniture and tasteful abstract paintings. She couldn't tell exactly who he was mocking, but he squeezed her hips as he joked, and so she didn't really care.

They made love twice a day. He was eager and athletic—moving her from room to room in their tiny suite—propping her against walls and flimsy pieces of antique furniture. It was affair sex, a little brave and a little desperate, always mimicking something spectacular.

When they returned to the city, Laurel waited one day, with the fidgety anticipation of a schoolgirl, for Sloane to respond. She would have received the first letter by now. She would tearfully confront John; maybe she would throw things. John would storm over to Laurel's apartment, angry, shouting at her. Or maybe he would make a single late-night phone call from the den in his huge, warm house. "What have you done?" he would whisper, heartbroken. She was unsure of what exactly would happen, so she waited, full of excited dread and a thickness in her chest that felt like lust.

But nothing happened. John called her at noon on Tuesday, and she left the hospital where she worked to meet him for lunch. They went to a Salvadoran place and ate pupusas, and he licked the grease from her fingers, slowly, his eyes focused on hers. Laurel realized Sloane hadn't said anything about the letter and felt a rush of pleasure. They had a secret. She and Sloane against John. It made her generous with him, and as they walked back to his car, she put her arm around his waist and leaned into him, fearlessly.

On Wednesday night, Laurel sent another letter:

Dear Sloane,

I shuffle these facts around in my mind all day long: He hates mushrooms. He won't wear yellow. He loves to shave but resents showers for the waste of time they are. He has, strangely enough, enormous affection for decrepit old dogs. One time we met in the park for lunch. It was one of those frustrating meetings when we were afraid to touch for fear of who might see us. We watched each other through a collection of shifty glances. There was a dog walker there with nearly a dozen old dogs in tow and John got the biggest kick out of it. He got down on his knees and ruffled their fur. He tried to engage them in chase and catch. Would he do that if he were at the park with you? I wonder if I were married to him, if his refusal to eat mushrooms would get on my nerves (I love them).

Did you get my last letter? If you did, you didn't say anything to John. I spoke to him yesterday (well, actually, I saw him, too) and he didn't mention it.

She walked to the end of the block and dropped the stiff envelope into the mailbox, then she rushed home, as if there could be some result waiting. She tried to watch TV. She tried to read a magazine. She ironed some blouses, quickly and badly. And then she gave up and wandered the three rooms of her apartment, sipping red wine and waiting. The expanse of her life had been squeezed into this moment, confined to the bursting point, so that of the spectrum of emotions, she could feel nothing but anticipation. Her heart thrummed and contracted and sent blood rushing to her cheeks.

Her phone rang, and she had to sit and breathe for a moment before she answered. It could be anybody, she told herself. It turned out to be a pollster, asking her about newspapers, whether she recognized the slogan "All the News That's Fit to Print." She answered the man's questions for fifteen minutes, glad for the conversation. When she hung up, it was silent again. She sat on her couch, balancing her wine glass on her knee, and stared. What other thing, she wondered, had ever made her feel so curious about what would happen next?

On Friday morning, John called at seven-thirty and told Laurel to call in sick. He would be over by nine. She did as she was asked, diagnosing herself with a head cold to the nurse on duty. She pictured her students, eagerly clutching their clipboards as they noted the amount of urine passed in the night or took a resting blood pressure. She was fond of them, of their practical studiousness and collective lack of imagination.

She showered quickly but didn't get dressed. Instead, she wrapped her old robe back around her and waited, combing her fingers through her thick wet hair.

She watched him from the living room window as he jogged down the street to her door. She liked his outline, the broad shoulders and square jaw, but now she noticed other things—she liked the way he ran, loose and full of confidence. She liked the vertical crease between his eyebrows, so deep she could see it from here. The buzzer rang like a grinding gear, and her heart did the little flip it had been waiting to do.

"What?" she said when he reached her door, an angry flirt.

"What?" he answered. He was breathing heavily from the stairs.

"What's so pressing that I had to skip work? One of my favorite patients gets discharged today and I'm going to miss saying goodbye." She didn't know why she said that. It wasn't true.

"Oh." His face pinching, "I just thought it would be fun to spend the day together. We could bum around the city or stay in and watch movies. I was being spontaneous." He said the last word expectantly, as if he weren't sure she would understand its meaning.

She backed up and let him in the door, but the air had turned heavy around her.

"I'll get dressed," she said. In her bedroom, she stood naked in front of the mirror. Her body looked lumpy and cold to her, full of dimples and rough patches. The morning was filling her, quickly and against her will with sadness.

When she was dressed, she found John in the kitchen, making a pot of coffee. She embraced him from behind, laying her cheek against his back to feel the warmth of his skin through his sweater. He turned in her arms and kissed her wetly on the lips.

As they made love, Laurel realized, with a sudden and embarrassed clarity, that she was faking. All of it, the kissing, the movements, the little groans of pleasure. On top of her, his body felt clammy and angular, his saliva cold.

She would propose a meeting. A place and a time. She would describe an outfit and then wear it, know Sloane from her red hair, the white Volvo. She smiled to herself, and John responded with renewed vigor.

It would go like this: Sloane would come, looking tired and exasperated but well put together. She would stop at the doorway. It would be a restaurant, a nice one with white tablecloths and wine glasses that reflected candlelight. Only when Sloane scanned the room would Laurel be able to detect her anxiousness. Sloane would sit across from Laurel, knowing her immediately from her youth and welcoming face, and sigh. Laurel would offer her a drink, and Sloane would order a glass of expensive red wine.

"Look," Laurel would say, "I know this is awkward, but I had to meet you. I wanted you to know…"

John made a high-pitched choking sound and collapsed beside her, smiling and panting. "I love you," he said. She smiled and buried her head against his chest.

And then she couldn't remember what it was she wanted Sloane to know. The fantasy seemed silly. Sloane would never meet her. She wouldn't even write back. Laurel had rented a P.O. box and written its address on the envelope. She checked it every day.

By noon, they were bored. They watched a movie and ordered in Chinese food that was limp and tasteless. The living room flickered, and the bright white light of day sliced through the curtains. Laurel felt restless. She looked at John clumsily slurping noodles from the box. His hair was matted and frizzy in the back from the brief nap he'd taken while she ordered food.

"Why do you think people have affairs?"

He looked at her, chopsticks perched before his mouth. Then he finished his bite, chewed it slowly, and put the box down. "What kind of question is that?"

"It's just a question-question. I thought as someone who's having an affair you might have some general insight as to why it's so prevalent."

"Look, I never planned to have an affair. I'm having one

because I met you, and I fell in love. I'm surprised by the whole thing, to tell you the truth."

Laurel raised her eyebrows and tucked her feet under her on the couch. The movie flickered on behind his head, creating a pulsing blue halo around him. She was supposed to feel flattered, she thought. What he expected was for her to melt off the couch and into his arms with gratitude. "Bullshit," she said, feeling just a little guilty as his face fell. "Really, in general, why do you think it is?"

John sighed like an exasperated schoolteacher—all these questions! "I suppose it's to fulfill something that's missing."

The corners of Laurel's mouth turned down as if to say, *maybe*. "It can't be just *something* missing. It must be something specific. Otherwise, why would you go about fulfilling it in this way? I mean, why not just leave the wife, or do something else? You could climb a mountain or take up guitar. Why an affair?" She knew she was treading into dangerous territory, that it almost sounded as if she were asking him to leave Sloane. She wasn't. She didn't know exactly what she was doing, but she knew it wasn't that.

"Come on," he said. "You're acting like a child. You know damn well I can't just up and leave Sloane. A marriage is a long and complicated thing. Besides, I love her. I mean," he looked at her pleadingly, "she's my wife; I do love her."

"Are you *in* love with her?" She hoped he would say yes but wasn't sure he knew how to save himself.

John frowned and blew a puff of air through his nose. "Look, we've been together for a long time. Things change. The nature of our relationship has changed."

"Just wondering," Laurel said. She got up off the couch and went into the bathroom for another shower. When she got out, John had straightened up the room. He was putting the food boxes in the refrigerator, rinsing glasses.

"Look, maybe today isn't the best day for us to be together. I think I'll just go to work and call you tomorrow."

She stood there with a towel wrapped around her body, water sending tickling rivulets down her shoulders, and felt sorrow click on, as if he had flicked a switch.

"All right," she said, going to him and kissing him on the cheek.

When he left, she got dressed and sat down to write.

Dear Sloane,

Do you know what it's like to be left? Not left like a husband leaves his wife but left like a man leaves his mistress. Every time is the very loneliest moment. When he leaves his mistress, it's always for another woman. And there is so little ground to stand on. Sometimes I can't remember what it was I loved about him. Do you know what it is you love about him? I miss him so much when he's gone.

Why don't you write me back?

> *Love,*
> *Laurel*

She folded the letter neatly and printed the address on the envelope. She felt spurned by Sloane, and as she walked to the mailbox, she was stopped in her steps by sudden images of Sloane and John sitting in the middle of their luscious king-sized bed laughing at the letters. If Sloane cared so little, why wouldn't she laugh? Maybe they were turning the whole thing into a good joke. Maybe, she imagined, she was being set up as the entertainment. A cruel and voyeuristic form of swinging.

After she dropped the letter in the mailbox, she went home filled with a blooming dread. It wasn't yet three, but she poured herself two fingers of whiskey and sat on the couch. This was just the kind of thing that made people crazy. Perhaps insanity wasn't doing the same things over and over and expecting different results. Perhaps insanity was just a collection of uncertainties with the imagination running wild to fill in the blanks.

She picked up the phone and dialed what she thought was their landline. When he answered, she was stunned. She had expected Sloane's voice. She tapped to hang up but continued to stare at the screen for a while. Thinking.

What would she have done if Sloane had answered? She had no plan. She simply wanted contact, to make sure they both existed and that she knew the path that connected them. Sometimes, when loneliness crushed her like sand, she imagined going there, just opening the door and going inside. It wasn't a break-up she wanted exactly, not a big scene, just to be noticed, to be seen, to be acknowledged in that house. The best thing would be to be kissed and asked inside.

She poured herself a sloppy second glass of whiskey, licking her fingers where the alcohol had sloshed out of the glass. Dusk was coming. The worst part of the day. It promised nothing, and the mere color of it made her anxious. She got up and walked around her apartment, turning on lights. When they were all burning, she sat down again. There was nothing to do. During the dim, cold afternoons of her childhood, she would sometimes lock herself in her bedroom and whisper one-sided conversations just to fill the space. She tried this now. She said, "Of course not," but had no idea why it had come out. Then she laughed, as if someone were watching.

Her car was parked down the street from her apartment. A light blue Honda she bought new for her college graduation eight years earlier. The ice cubes in her glass jingled as she fumbled in her purse for the keys.

"Fuck them," she said, jamming the key into the lock and opening the door.

The route from her neighborhood to theirs took her through the skinny strip of green in the park and up the voluptuous hills of San Francisco. As she crested each one, a view would open to her, lights and then the bay beyond, black and motionless, and then she would descend again into a trough lined on either side by crumbling Victorians, like dusty wedding cakes all in a row.

When she pulled up in front of his house on the quiet street where people paid to have their lawns cut and agreed to color coordinate their trim paint, she stared at the lights glowing from inside. They were yellow and warm, as if the interior of the house were a sunny place, separate from the fog-filled evening outside, as distant and alluring as the tropics. It was silent except for the pinging of the engine. Laurel sipped what was left of her whiskey.

The front door opened, letting all that golden light spill outside, and Sloane emerged, casually slinging a purse over her shoulder. She wasn't the formidable matron Laurel had imagined. She was petite and delicate, and her red hair swirled around her face like a girl's. Her eyes swept the sidewalk and street in front of her house without seeing, and Laurel thought of ducking. As Sloane walked down the front path, full of easy purpose—she was on her way to the grocery store, the dry cleaners—her eyes caught Laurel's and focused. She faltered for a moment, smiling, frowning, and smiling again, and approached the car. It was the kind of neighborhood where people noticed eight-year-old blue Hondas, where the residents exerted their entitlement over strangers.

"Can I help you?" she mouthed through the closed window.

Laurel willed her body not to betray her, not to let the wild-eyed helplessness show. She shook her head.

Sloane looked at her again, studying her face, then she motioned for Laurel to roll down the window.

Laurel leaned across the empty passenger seat, jabbing her rib on the emergency brake, and opened it wide. Cold, damp air flooded in.

"You're Laurel," Sloane said, and Laurel managed to nod, flinching slightly as if she were expecting a blow. Sloane straightened, took a deep breath, and then bent toward the window again. "I want you to stop it. I don't know what's wrong with you, but just stop it. What are you thinking? What could you possibly be thinking?"

Laurel looked straight ahead through the windshield at the darkening street before her. "I don't know," she said. The whiskey swirled in her brain; she felt dizzy. "I just wanted to know that you got them. I needed to know they got to you."

"I throw them away," Sloane said. "I want you to stop it." She had straightened up and spoke not into the window but out into the night.

"I will," Laurel said. "I just wanted to know you got them. I'll stop."

Sloane turned, walked back to her driveway, and started the Volvo.

When she'd driven away, Laurel started her car, aware of the noise it made in that empty, quiet neighborhood. Her breaths floated away from her like ghosts. Her heart beat itself against her breast. It was, she thought, like flying: all thrills and weightlessness, the body's predictable responses. "This is living," she said. "I am alive."

THE PERSON I SUSPECT I AM

I'M CLEANING OUT THE kitchen, getting rid of all the things that make my wife gag on sight. She's sitting in the living room, and I shout out the names of things I'm unsure of.

"Swiss Miss hot chocolate with mini marshmallows," I yell.

"Ugh," Ruthie says, like a moan.

I'm a little sad to see some of it go. Other things make me strangely ashamed of myself—I'm sure I bought the Swiss Miss, for example, and it seems cheap and childish and in very bad taste now that I see it among the beautifully packaged organic pastas and little jars of capers and tapenade.

My wife is two months pregnant and hugely sick. I throw away whatever she wants me to because she's the one who has to throw up and cry and smell every foul thing usually undetectable by the human nose.

Because we're thirty-five, we're not really allowed to tell anyone about the pregnancy for another month or so. The only people who know are my brother Nick and Ruthie's best friend, Isabel, and probably his girlfriend and her husband, but we aren't sure about that.

It hasn't proven to be a difficult secret to keep. I'm the only one who knows about her retching, and sometimes, as I stand over her at four in the morning, holding her hair away from her face as she gags into the toilet bowl, I think I've never felt closer to anyone. There's a part of me that wants to keep this our secret forever. I realize, of course, that that's impossible.

I'm putting the grocery bags full of the unwanted food into the garage when my phone rings. It's Nick, a day early. He's an hour away, he says, and I hear the thunder of trucks speeding by whatever roadside he is standing on. He tells me he'll be here in a bit, that he can't wait to see us. I'm smiling when I hang up the phone, but I suddenly feel very rushed.

I haven't seen my brother in over nine months, since right before he left on his road trip to Costa Rica. I've received a few emails: one telling me he ate some sort of jungle rodent in El Salvador and one telling me that he and Beth-Ann broke up in Managua and that she was flying back to Seattle while he pushed on. In my mind's eye, my brother's progress down the isthmus of Central America is like a hardware store paint chip, a slowly ascending spectrum of green that begins with the mottled grassy-beige of California and ends up in the brilliant emerald of the Costa Rican jungle. In the movie of his life, I hear chirping, see flashes of the psychedelic wing of some seldom-seen tropical bird. His soundtrack is a mixture of Grateful Dead and the salsa music I sometimes listen to in the car when I'm driving alone.

In the living room I find Ruthie lying on her back on the couch with her hands resting lightly on her still-flat belly.

"I don't care about birth defects; I want the anti-nausea drugs," she says.

"How about a baked potato instead?"

"No thanks. Was that Nick?"

"Yeah. He's early. He'll be here in about an hour."

My wife opens her eyes and smiles. "Oh good," she says. "He'll take my mind off my goddamned stomach."

Nick looks like some hippie Viking back from conquering the

world. I'm never able to get used to the way he looks and now, as if on cue, I'm once again, for the millionth time, taken aback by his height and his blondness and his pure master-of-the-universe presence. Once, in college, my girlfriend at the time was trying to soothe me during one of my many youth-induced anxiety attacks by saying, "I think it's normal to feel insecure when you have a brother who looks like an absolute *Greek god.*"

Nick is dressed in baggy green pants patched here and there with brightly colored pieces of fabric. He has an intricately embroidered vest on over his bare torso, and he is exceedingly tan. I find myself thinking about how easy it must be for him to get laid.

We embrace in the doorway, patting each other heartily between the shoulder blades. He hangs on, giving me one of those long, earnest hugs that make men like me uncomfortable.

"Where's the little mama?" he asks when we part.

"I'm in here, trying not to vomit. Come hug me," Ruthie yells from the couch.

Nick bounds toward her on the balls of his feet like a basketball player. I close the front door and carry his bag into his room. By the time I enter the living room, Nick is sitting on the couch next to Ruthie's knees with his hands spread out over her stomach like a diviner. They both have their eyes closed, and I stand silently, watching them, feeling as if I'm interrupting.

Ruthie's eyes open and she looks at Nick. "I actually *do* feel better. Roger," she says, turning to me. "I feel much better. Shall we try to go to lunch?"

Nick doesn't shower, but he does throw a T-shirt on under his vest before we leave. His truck is parked in front of the building.

"That," he says, pointing to the crumpled front fender, "was a very unfortunate burro."

"My god." Ruthie says, splaying a hand over her heart. "Did it die?"

"It was pretty bad. I broke both its front legs. I ended up having to shoot it and then tow it off into a ditch with the truck.

That was in Mexico. Beth-Ann was freaked."

"You carried a gun?" I ask.

"Only after Saltillo," he says, smiling.

We take our car, a new "champagne" Subaru with leather seats.

"So, what is it now, like a kidney bean?" Nick asks Ruthie once she's buckled up.

"Something like that. It has a heartbeat, though. Isn't that amazing? A tiny, tiny heart the size of a poppy seed." Ruthie is twisting in her seat, looking at Nick.

"Can you feel it?"

"Only if it feels like the stomach flu."

"She throws up every day. A couple of times," I offer.

"Man," Nick says. "You're a brave woman." He stares out the window for a moment. "You know, I spent a couple of nights in this clinic in Honduras and assisted the doctor with a birth. This lady, she was thirty-eight and giving birth to her fourteenth child. When it came out, she just rolled over and shooed us away. She didn't even want to hold it."

Ruthie sighs. "Sometimes it seems so unfair. You know what this pregnancy cost us? Five grand. Five thousand dollars and our sex life."

Heat spreads across my chest and up to my face. I think about the night we conceived. I think it was the same night she said to me, as I kissed her neck, "Could you maybe try to do this quickly? I can tell I'm not going to get into it this time."

In the month since the test came back positive, we have only tried sex a couple of times. We've been distracted and tired, going at each other in a perfunctory manner and then falling asleep irritated and impatient. One morning last week, I heard Ruthie laughing, telling Isabel on the phone, "I don't know what's wrong with me, but let me tell you, I would have fucked a lemon if I thought it would give me an orgasm." I haven't been able to get that picture out of my head. My wife fucking a lemon. It seems vaguely Scandinavian.

Nick says, "Man. America's such a trip." And just when I feel the familiar tightness coming over me, just when I'm once and for all sick of my brother and his relentless coolness, we arrive at the restaurant and Nick kisses the back of my head and says, "This is too cool."

The day after our mother's funeral, I graduated from college. It was understood our father would not come, that he was too fragile with grief and relief to be asked to do anything. My graduation seemed trivial in the face of her big black casket and all those crying aunts and the great, empty yawn of our mother's absence from the rest of our lives.

I walked somberly through the ceremony while all around me my classmates cheered and passed joints and bottles of champagne. As I stepped off the stage, diploma in hand, I was surprised to see Nick there, focusing the lens of his camera on my face.

"I know this seems stupid now, but someday you're going to want to remember that this happened too," he said to me, clicking the shutter.

We went out to a bar after that—some dive where we would not come across any celebrating graduates. We ordered hamburgers and got incredibly, dizzyingly drunk. We toasted all night, clinking the dense shot glasses of tequila together. To Mom. To graduation. To Dad. To brotherhood. To women, especially ones who were nice to us. To orphans. To Jackie, the family beagle, dead for twelve years.

By the time I woke in the morning, feeling poisoned, perched at death's door, Nick was gone on his way to Alaska where a fishing boat job would fall through, forcing him to spend his summer in the muck of a fish cannery separating guts from flesh.

He doesn't know how long he's staying. Maybe a week, maybe two, he says. He sleeps in the office, which we're planning to turn into the nursery soon, even though Ruthie is reading a book on something called "attachment parenting" and insists that the baby will sleep with us and won't need its own room for at least a couple of years.

When I leave for work in the mornings, Nick is still sleeping. Ruthie shushes me, tiptoeing exaggeratedly so I'll get the point.

"You're going to have to learn to be quiet, anyway," she says, pointing to her abdomen.

When I come home, I often find Nick standing barefoot in the kitchen cooking dinner. He makes single pot dishes. Beans and rice flavored with curry or hot sauce or some Cajun spice he claims is a secret. Ruthie, who has subsisted on baked potatoes and cottage cheese for a month, eats slowly, taking tiny, baby bites until her plate is empty.

I've become accustomed to watching my wife throw up, to seeing the partially digested remains of her dinner float in the toilet bowl like mosaics. Now, when we stumble together, sleepy-eyed, into the bathroom, I wonder if my brother can hear us. This has become our intimate nighttime ritual, and I've started turning on the bathroom faucet full blast in the hopes of drowning out the sounds of my wife retching and of me offering helpless assurances of my love as she does so.

One day, I come home to find Ruthie in a huge lavender dress, swishing and posing like a runway model. Nick's sitting on the couch, watching the show. When she sees me, she stops and bends over, laughing.

"What do you think?" she asks. "We went to the mall. I bought my first maternity dress." She plucks at the front of the dress, pulling it out from her stomach.

"It'll be a while before you need it," I say. "But it's nice. It'll look good on you."

"It just felt so incredibly soft. Nick doesn't get the whole shopping thing, but I felt like it was a lucky dress."

"It's nice," I say again, but I can feel it's not enough. "I definitely feel its lucky powers," I say, but Ruthie just rolls her eyes at me.

"You guys don't get it." She disappears into the bedroom and comes back wearing a T-shirt and jeans. She looks beautiful and when she joins us at the table, I feel so proud of her.

On Saturday, after Nick's been with us a week, I drive down the coast with him to watch him surf because he asks me to. The beach is swathed in fog, but as we stand on the damp sand, we can see the black heads of surfers bobbing beyond the break. The waves are big and messy, breaking and roiling for yards and yards until they reach the beach. Nick stands beside me in his wetsuit, his surfboard tucked under his arm.

"Well," he says, "nothing ventured…" He bounds down the slope of sand and splashes into the water.

I watch as he paddles himself through the froth, ducking as waves crash and roll over him. It takes twenty minutes before he is out with the other surfers and when I look away, I lose him. He is one of those black heads rising and falling with the swells, but I can't pick him out. I watch for his tall silhouette to appear, gliding toward me on his board, but none of them look like Nick.

I'm freezing in the fog. My sweatshirt is flapping in the wind, and it feels as if all my clothes are damp. I sit on the cold sand and scan the horizon, trying to pick Nick out of the cluster of anonymous, identical heads above the waves.

The longer I sit, the angrier I become. It's fucking freezing on the beach and as the moisture seeps through the butt of my jeans, I imagine what I'll say when Nick finally shows up, floating out of the gloom. It's been over an hour, and I've long since stopped watching the ocean. I stare at the sand, poking little holes with a stick, screaming at Nick in my mind. This is just so goddamned typical, I imagine myself saying to his grinning, feline face. What makes you think it's interesting for me to sit and freeze my ass off while you float around shooting the shit with a bunch of stoners? Does he even know about the sharks, about how many people have drowned out there? In my reverie I'm so mad my face is red and spit flies from my lips as I yell.

I don't even notice Nick standing above me, dripping into the sand until he says, "If it's a girl, you should name her Georgia, after Mom."

I look up at him, stunned out of my daydream by my brother's actual physical presence.

"It's good because every little girl in her kindergarten won't be named Georgia, plus it's a cute name for a little girl, don't you think?" He's jerking his head to the side, trying to unplug his ear. "Brrr. Man, it was freezing out there. I need calories. Burrito?"

We walk back across the dark sand to the parking lot, and I sit in the car as Nick strips out of his wetsuit and gets back into the pants he's been wearing for five days. When he gets in, he says, "You should take up surfing. The waves here are good to learn on."

I start the car with a roar. "It's not really my thing," I say.

We drive in silence back toward the city. Nick is fiddling with the radio and settles on an NPR interview with some blues musician.

When we pull up in front of Taqueria Cancun, he turns to me and says, "Is something the matter, man? Are you mad at me or something?"

I yank the emergency brake into place and sigh. "No, I'm not mad at you," I say. "I was just freezing to death out there, that's all."

Nick smiles and slaps my shoulder. "That's why you should surf, man. It's always better to do than to watch." He gets out, rubs a towel roughly through his hair, and goes into the taqueria. This makes me want to punch him, to cram his mouth full of one of his tattered Guatemalan rags until he can no longer speak.

After nine days, Nick tells us over dinner that he'll be leaving the day-after-tomorrow. He's going to visit friends in Colorado, climb some mountain, and be back in Boulder for a world music festival he's been hoping to attend. He's not sure where he's going to settle. Beth-Ann kept their apartment in Seattle, so not there. Maybe Montana or Idaho, somewhere he can get a job fighting wildfires, somewhere where he can live in a tent until he saves up enough money to rent shelter for the winter. He tells us this while he scoops big spoonfuls of fiery chorizo casserole into his mouth, filling his cheeks like a chipmunk while he talks.

I feel a pang I mistake for disappointment and then, looking at my impossibly confident brother, this guy who acquires guns in Mexico and uses them on donkeys and knows the dates and whereabouts of music festivals and other gatherings of groovy people, I properly identify the pang as jealousy. A wormy, guilty jealousy, not of his travels or his good looks or the easy way he forms friendships with everybody, but of the fact that he is always the one who gets to say how it's going to be. I sit silently wishing that I hadn't waited for him to announce his departure but had orchestrated it myself. We have a life to get on with. My wife, after all, is pregnant and sick and in need of her rest.

Ruthie says, "Oh shoot. No more afternoon poker games. I was getting good." Since the pregnancy, Ruthie has stopped taking freelance jobs. I don't begrudge her. Or I didn't.

Nick looks at me. "It's true. I owe her something like a million dollars."

"I didn't know you two were playing poker."

"Yep," Ruthie says, taking one of her miniscule bites, "I've always wanted to learn, and it takes my mind off my stomach for a while. Turns out, I'm sort of good at it."

"Well, you and I can play in the evenings. I don't know how

I'll be now, but back in grad school I certainly won a lot of matchsticks." I can hear how awful I sound, and even as these impotent sentences leave my lips, I regret them. Sometimes I'm scared I'm the person I suspect I am.

"Okay," she says, shrugging.

That night, as Ruthie is vomiting, Nick knocks on the bathroom door.

"Ruthie," he calls softly through the door, "remember what I told you about breathing. Try the butterfly breath when you're done." My wife nods once and continues to barf.

When we're back in bed, I lie in the dark listening to Ruthie take long, deep breaths and exhale them with a stutter. This, I suppose, is the butterfly breath, something Nick no doubt learned in the jungles of Indonesia or from a medicine man he broke bread with on some far-off scorching plain.

I whisper into the dark, "Are you in love with my brother?"

Ruthie stops her breathing mid-flutter. "Are you insane? No. You're my husband."

"It just seems like you two get along so well. It seems like you like having him around."

"We do. I do. But once every six months or so is about what I can take. You know Nick. He's great, but he's a bit much. God, Roger. When did you get so jealous?"

"I don't know," I say. "Nick makes me feel insecure."

"Well, get over it," she whispers into the dark. "It's unbecoming."

We have no idea when it started but by the time the alarm goes off at six-thirty, there is a dark circle of blood on the sheet. Ruthie wakes up when I do and says, "Oh my God," as she sits up, examining the sticky wetness on her nightgown. "This isn't it. This better not be it," she says. She's clutching my arm, digging the pads of her fingers into the soft under part. The room takes on a rippled, watery effect, and for a moment, it's unclear to me whether or not this is a dream.

"What do we do?" I ask. "Do we go to the hospital?"

My wife moans and digs her fingers deeper into my arm. "It hurts," she says. "Oh God, I think this is it."

Bile rises and burns in my throat as I pull on some clothes and help Ruthie into her big soft maternity dress.

By the time we get out of the car in the hospital parking lot, Ruthie's dress is soaked through with blood. Wait, I tell her, while I run in for a wheelchair.

"My wife," I tell the nurses, panting, "My wife is having a miscarriage." The word catches in my throat. But the nurses are unmoved. They point without expression to a group of wheelchairs in the corner.

I'm breathing hard, doing my own version of the butterfly breath as I run across the parking lot pushing the wheelchair. In the gray light of morning, the parking lot seems endless, like something out of a nightmare. When I reach the car, I see Ruthie sitting in the passenger seat, her head back, her eyes closed.

When I open the door, she opens her eyes. "I can't believe this is happening," she says.

The doctor, a woman with a perky blond ponytail and red clogs examines Ruthie and says, "Yep. You're having a miscarriage. Looks like you already passed most of it, but we'll clean you out just the same." She is bizarrely chipper. It's like being told by a cheerleader you've lost your baby.

Ruthie chews on her lower lip like a little girl while she lies on the gurney waiting to be wheeled into the room where I will not be allowed to follow. She's in a hospital gown, and I ask her what she wants me to do with the dress, which is stiff with drying blood and lying in a paper grocery bag at my feet.

"Throw it away," she says. "It was stupid of me to buy it."

When the orderlies come to take her away, I hurry to find the proper receptacle for the dress, and as I shove it into the tiny trashcan/ashtray outside the emergency room doors, I wonder if it contains the kidney bean of a fetus, and if so, if it deserves a more dignified disposal. I take the dress out of the trash can, careful not to unfold it—I don't want to see anything, any little mass of flesh—and I put it back in the bag. I decide I'll burn it, and I hurry back to the car and shove the bag underneath the driver's seat where Ruthie won't see it.

The last of the morning traffic dissipates in the drizzle as we drive home. Ruthie is wearing a hospital gown and a pink robe they gave her, something left behind by grieving relatives is what I suspect. She's resting her head against the window, watching. We're holding hands across the center of the car, and I'm trying to rub some warmth back into her fingertips.

When we get home, Nick's in the kitchen. "Wherever you were, I hope you bought OJ," he yells when he hears the door open. He comes out, shirtless and grinning, and meets us in the hall. "Rog," he says, surprised to see me. "What's up? I'm making breakfast." Then he looks at Ruthie and notices what she's wearing and how she looks.

"It's gone," she says, looking at the floor. She rolls her eyes and lets out a mirthless laugh as if she's embarrassed.

Nick enfolds Ruthie in his arms, holding her against his bare chest and she cries great, vocal sobs like a child. I step toward them unsure, and then I wrap myself around her back, encircling my arms around her and grabbing my brother at the waist so we're standing with her between us in what our mother would have called a "Ruthie sandwich." I feel Ruthie's back heave against me, and I kiss the back of her head, her shoulders, the freezing tips of her ears. We stay like that for a while, until Ruthie stops shaking and squirms free.

"Come on," Nick says, holding our hands and guiding us into

the kitchen. He sits us down at the table and then sweeps his hand above it, "Sorry about this," he says. "I didn't know."

The table is set for breakfast. Laid with fruit and muffins and a carton of milk. He begins to clear it away, embarrassed, I assume, by its cheeriness.

"Don't," Ruthie says, "I'm starving. Leave it."

Nick sits with us and sighs. "I knew a healer in Arizona—" he says, but Ruthie cuts him off.

"Not now, Nick," she says. She's eating a muffin, breaking off little crumbly bits of it and poking them into her mouth. "Let's just be quiet for a while."

I sit across from her, watching as she finishes her muffin and begins to peel a banana. Underneath my sadness something shimmers with the ominous beauty of a gasoline slick and I recognize it immediately as relief.

THE UNCERTAINTY PRINCIPLE

THE LECTURE IS BORING, and I've already leaned over and whispered into Leon's ear that I think so. But he has more patience than I, and I can tell by the way he scowls toward the stage that he's annoyed with me for being so restless. I'm petulantly folding my arms, preparing to pout my way through the rest of "Chaos, String Theory, and the Little-Known Universe" when the room begins to shudder. At first a great groan comes up and I think for an instant that I may have missed an important comment from one of the panelists. But then the vibration quickens and there is a chattering and a tinkling and before I think about it, I look at Leon and say "earthquake" as if to confirm the obvious. This is in the moment before action, when everyone freezes to see if it's worth standing up or taking cover. One doesn't want to seem panicky. Calm during earthquakes is a great indicator of one's place in this state. It's like a fancy zip code, a discreet measurement of belonging.

The crowd realizes the seriousness of this particular quake all at once and like a giant wave, it rises and begins to head for the aisles. There are screams, many nervous hooting noises, some swearing. The scientists on stage are ripping the lavalier mics from their lapels and jogging awkwardly into the wings. Leon and I are just standing up, frozen in a forward crouch, when a loud, cacophonous chiming causes me to look up and see the enormous, sparkling chandelier detach itself from the domed ceiling of the auditorium and fall as if it is being pulled earthward by something much stronger than gravity. I feel fear for the first time in the last seven seconds, and then I feel as if my arm is being ripped from its socket as the edge of the chandelier grates down the side of it and lands, with a deafening, shattering crash, on my boyfriend's head. He disappears into the shards of crystal and glass, one tweed arm emerging limply from the mess.

My arm burns in a numb, painless way and then I scramble over the seats behind me, hiking up my skirt and crawling like Jackie Kennedy did in Dallas, landing on my elbows in the aisle and then pushing myself up and running toward the exit. The room is still shaking; we will find out later that the earthquake lasted a little over forty-nine seconds, a lifetime.

People are really screaming now, throwing elbows and falling down in their hurry to get out of the theater. Pieces of gilded plaster are falling from the balcony, the little fingers of cherubs raining down in a pelting, golden cloud.

I've reached the foyer when the shaking stops, but it takes me and everyone else a few seconds to understand the stillness. When we do, there is an edgy slowing down. We're like rabbits taking a rest, all twitching jaws and tensed muscles. Then a deep voice booms from the crowd asking us to please remain calm and exit the building in an orderly fashion. People are still streaming in from the auditorium and the foyer is thick with the dusty members of the scientific community and their companions.

I can't get my lower jaw to stop chattering. I feel like a rabid dog, like I might start growling and drooling and acting dangerous. But I don't. I stay where I am, stepping from foot to foot, trying not to bite my tongue. I don't exit the foyer. I can't. Outside the glass doors I can see red lights reflected in the wet street. Sirens wail from all over the city, hundreds of scurrying bodies are running down the sidewalk. So much for earthquake weather, I think, watching the drizzle hurl itself into the headlights of stopped cars.

Leon is dead, I'm sure of it, but I can't do anything about it at the moment. I'm aware in a buzzing, peripheral kind of way that this is going to end up being the worst thing that has ever happened to me, that I will suffer and never fully recover, but I'm too busy keeping myself from acting like a rabid dog to react properly. I see the limp, tweed-wrapped arm over and over again, the one I've slept against for seven years, ever since I graduated and it became more or less okay for me to move in with Leon, and each time, I shake my head, trying to dislodge that image.

Dr. Paul Wolof, one of Leon's colleagues, a new guy recently transferred from the University of Indiana, approaches and takes my elbow. His fingers are moist and tentative against my skin. I notice him slowly, his weak chin, his round, brown face, his corona of dusty hair.

"Are you all right?" he asks, and it is only then that I realize that other people are starting to calm down. I see a woman smiling and rolling her eyes, and I get the impression she's making fun of herself for being so scared. The residents of San Francisco are quick to out-blasé one another, and as I look around, the crowd begins to look more and more like a cocktail party, like one of those horrible department socials I sometimes go to with Leon, the ones full of scientists who make me ashamed of being a sculptor, whose very presence makes the words "textile art" sound frivolous and West Coasty, on par with astrology or the raw food movement.

I look at Dr. Wolof, my jaw still chattering away and say, "Leon's dead."

He blanches and frowns. The general mood in the foyer is that everything has turned out just fine. "He was crushed by the chandelier, the giant one in the middle."

Dr. Wolof lets go of my arm and rushes away, jogging back into the auditorium. I like that he's done that. It seems normal and capable. Maybe I had him pegged all wrong, I think, as I watch his blue oxford disappear.

While he's gone, I turn my attention back to the big glass front doors. People are leaving now and because the doors are open, the sounds of the city's sirens are louder. The air is cold and damp. Traffic goes nowhere.

Some people have the constitution for things like this, some dormant and untapped source of strength. But I don't. I have nothing that hasn't already been tapped; I use every bit of inner strength I have just to get through regular life and I have no reserves for emergency situations. Which, I realize, is part of the reason I'm still with Leon almost a year after he lost interest in me and started having an affair with one of his graduate students, a girl named Beverly from Cut Bank, Montana, who has, I've been told, an amazing mind for solar physics.

The foyer, which moments ago was full of warm, panicky bodies, is starting to empty. But I stay where I am, still rocking from foot to foot and waiting for Dr. Wolof to come back. I can't bring myself to leave because of my aforementioned lack of inner strength, and because Leon had the car keys, and because I don't even know if driving is a possibility. The Golden Gate Bridge could have fallen into the ocean for all I know. This is what we imagine when we imagine a great tragedy in this city.

Plus, there's the question of the house, which is across the bridge and built on a hill prone to losing great chunks of itself in the rainy season. The house could be a pile of matchsticks at the bottom of the ravine. So I'm stuck in the foyer with my cortisol induced shakes.

Dr. Wolof jogs in from the auditorium. He's frowning and breathing heavily and when he reaches me, he frowns so hard his eyebrows touch in the middle.

"He's not in there," he says, taking long, catch-up breaths.

"He's under the chandelier. The big one in the center."

"Could someone have already gotten him out?' He tries to look sympathetic, but I can tell he's beginning to regret coming to my aid.

"It's only been five minutes. I was standing right next to him and then … boom. I ran."

"Well, he's not there now."

"Look for his arm. His arm is sticking out. The rest of him is under all that crystal."

Dr. Wolof lets out a big puff of air. His breath is minty fresh. "Look, Rosie," he says. "He's just not there. I looked. I'll take you back in there if you want."

My heart does a little contraction. I don't want to go back in there, to witness the scene of that previous horror. I don't want to look at Leon's limp arm again. I shake my head.

He sighs again. "Here, let me take you home."

"I'm scared it fell down. We're on a hill, a steep one. I have this feeling it just tumbled into the ravine."

"Why don't I take you back to my house then, and we can see about Leon. We can call the hospitals, see if someone got him there without you seeing it."

I let myself be led out the glass front doors, because despite his appearance—soft, hopelessly nerdy, virginal—I'm fully convinced of Dr. Wolof's competence.

We're walking up Van Ness. There are no lights on except what's coming from the stopped cars. People have gotten out and are directing traffic. It's misting heavily and tiny beads of moisture collect on my face and on the soft fluff of Dr. Wolof's afro.

"Did you know Wolof is an African language?" I say, as we hurry up the street, heads bent down.

"Yes. Part of the Niger-Congo language family. Spoken mostly in Senegal but also in Gambia," he says, without taking his eyes off the cracked and buckled sidewalk.

"I used to know how to say 'I'm really stoned' in Wolof, but I forget now."

Dr. Wolof glances at me and his eyebrows jump together briefly. "Can you say anything in Wolof?" I ask.

"No. I've never been to West Africa."

I trip over a chunk of cement, and Dr. Wolof catches me by the elbow to keep me from falling. He lets go again, and we say nothing for a while.

We've gone two long blocks in search of his car when I say, "Where do you live? Maybe we should walk."

He looks around, jingling the keys in his pocket and noticing for the first time that driving will be impossible; people have abandoned their cars in the middle of the street.

"You're probably right, but it's a hike."

I shrug. Walking feels good. I've stopped shivering and I'm able to fill my lungs. We cross the street and head east. North Beach, I think. Maybe Nob Hill.

When we cross Polk Street, we find people clustered outside the bars, drinks still in their hands. Huge drag queens in sparkling hot pants and platform shoes lean against buildings, smoking cigarettes and sipping from martini glasses. Everyone is outside, lit by the glow of headlights and brake lights and the flickering emergency fluorescents of a few of the buildings. A man with a thick blond moustache runs up and thrusts a bottle of champagne at me. I accept it and take a great, fizzing gulp. "Fuckin-A," he says, grinning.

"Fuckin-A," I say back. I return the bottle, forgetting to offer it to Dr. Wolof.

We've passed Polk Street and are heading uphill into the residential neighborhood when I say, "Where *have* you been?"

Dr. Wolof stops. "What?"

I face him, breathing hard. "You said you'd never been to West Africa, so where have you been?"

His eyebrows are really doing their thing now. "Why are you asking me now? This is a state of emergency. Your...um, your *partner* may be dead. I think you need to focus a little."

"Do you know a woman named Beverly? Have you ever had her as a student?"

A blush rises in his face and he shakes his head. "I know who she is."

"She's really smart, huh?"

"She has gained some notoriety within the department for having an exceptional mind for conceptual physics."

I make a mental note. *Conceptual*, not solar. Or maybe both.

"Leon says I have emotional intelligence. That's a physicist's way of saying you're dumb. It's a euphemism." A long fire engine passes us, wailing along with its many counterparts throughout the city. They're like whales communicating in a strange language across vast distances. We stop talking, and I plug my ears with my index fingers.

When the fire engine is gone, I say, "It *is* true that I barely passed physics, even with Leon as my teacher. In some ways, I don't even want to know how things work. I think the mystery is more poetic. I mean I hope they discover a cure for cancer, and I like email and everything. It's just that—."

"Rosie!" Dr. Wolof says sharply. But when I look up, I can tell he's embarrassed to have shouted. He clears his throat. "Let's keep walking. We still have at least ten more blocks."

We trudge up the hill, through the mist, without speaking. People are standing outside the gates to their buildings talking to one another and exchanging stories. No one seems to be panicked or hurt. I find their presence calming. If it's still possible to stand outside on the sidewalk and shoot the shit with the neighbors, then there's a chance life can get back to normal. Maybe my house is even still standing. Maybe Leon is even alive, although I find this hard to believe. His arm.

Dr. Wolof lives on the border between Chinatown and North Beach in a building that houses both a bank and a donut shop on the ground floor. The windows of both are broken but no one's inside. A security guard stands outside sipping milk from one of those mini cartons. Dr. Wolof asks if the building is safe, and the security guard shrugs and says, "It's an at-your-own-risk situation at this point."

Dr. Wolof fumbles with his keys, and we enter the dark

building. "No elevator, I guess," he says. We make our way up the stairs, holding tight to the cold, metal banister. It's the kind of dark our eyes will never adjust to. No light at all. "This must be what a black hole feels like," I say. He emits a puff of air through his nose. Something between a laugh and a scoff.

We walk up four invisible floors and then enter a hallway and feel our way down the wall until he finds his door, fumbles again with the keys, and opens it into his apartment. Weak light glows through the windows, absolutely brilliant compared to the hallway.

"Have a seat. I'll find some candles."

"They don't recommend that," I say, surveying the room. "The worst thing about the 1906 quake wasn't the shaking, but the fires afterwards."

He pauses and then goes into the kitchen, leaving me in the living room, which is nothing special, neither messy nor particularly neat. The furniture doesn't match but neither is it sloppy or cheap. There's a brown, nubby couch, a lamp with a red ceramic base sitting on the side table, some beige throw pillows. The coffee table is littered with opened bills and a coffee cup and the walls, under the corner windows, are lined with books. I strain from my seat on the couch to see what they are, but I can't read the spines in this light. Dr. Wolof comes back with a flashlight that shines a dim circle of yellow onto the hardwood floor. He uses it to locate an enormous phone book and then sits across from me in a leather chair and balances a landline phone on his knees. "We should start with General," he says, brushing through the thin phone book pages quickly. They crackle loudly as he searches. I watch him. Who has a phone book? A landline?

"You're so prepared."

He doesn't look up. "I have a hard time throwing away things I think might come in handy one day."

My nose is running from the cold and every time I sniffle Dr. Wolof looks at me to make sure I haven't started crying. I want to tell him he doesn't have to worry. I feel as hollow and stone-faced as a doll. It's shock, I presume. Outside, the city is still filled with the sounds of sirens wailing.

I watch as he dials the number of San Francisco General and then goes through a series of prompts, impatiently pressing buttons and sighing. I don't know what news I want to hear and although Leon was crushed by the chandelier right before my eyes, I'm starting to doubt my understanding of the events preceding this moment. It's difficult now to even remember what the earthquake felt like, to believe that it was real and that the earth, the whole humming city, was shuddering and shaking beneath us less than an hour ago.

"Hi," I hear Dr. Wolof say finally. "I'm searching for a missing person. Leon Rummel. He was at the Herbst Theater." Dr. Wolof says "uh-huh" a couple of times and then starts snapping his fingers at me and pointing behind me. He wants a pen, and I get him one from the jar on the telephone table in the hall. He scribbles a number on the cover of the phone book and hangs up. "They don't know anything. We're supposed to call a central emergency number. It sounded pretty hectic down there. I wish the electricity was on; I want to see what's happening."

I remember the wind-up radio I bought for Leon's last birthday. We keep it under the bed in case of the Big One and now, if the house is still standing, it's still there, waiting for someone to finally put it to its proper use. This makes me sad. I don't want Leon to be dead. Even if he ends up leaving me for Beverly and her marvelous mind, I at least want him to be alive.

Dr. Wolof dials the emergency number and waits through another series of prompts. He waits a bit more and then pushes a button and an instrumental version of "One of Us" by Joan Osborne comes through the receiver. We're on hold.

He puts the receiver back in its cradle and the music continues to fill the dark space between us. We are amazingly alone in his small apartment, four stories above a disaster that will go down in history, that my future children will someday learn about in school. Outside there are still occasional shouts and a few people honking their horns, trying in vain to get traffic moving.

"What if we were the last people alive in the whole city, walking through the ruins like some visiting archeologist, like Charlton Heston in *Planet of the Apes*?"

Dr. Wolof plants his hands on his knees and pushes himself up. "Do you want some crackers and cheese? I'm starving."

I shrug and nod at the same time. Whatever. Dr. Wolof is tired of me, I can tell. I can hear myself sounding weird. "Detached" is how Leon explains these moods, but I can't help it. I feel physically incapable of focusing, of bending my mind toward understanding this moment. I really do want Dr. Wolof to imagine *Planet of the Apes* with me, stepping through the ruins of restaurants we know, and libraries, and the halls of the university, but he won't. He will only do the right thing, sit quietly through instrumental versions of mid-90s pop hits until he gets the information he's after. Like Leon, Dr. Wolof is patient.

He returns with a box of Wheat Thins and a hunk of cheddar with the plastic wrapping pulled back to expose the orange rectangle. "There's some wine, too," he says, setting the cutting board down on the coffee table between us and heading back into the kitchen.

He comes back with the wine and two glasses held upside down between his fingers. It's a waiter's trick, and I try for a second to imagine Dr. Wolof as a waiter, all smiles and winking pleasantries. This is difficult because I don't recall ever having seen Dr. Wolof smile. He pours us each a glass and then sits back down in his chair facing me.

"You're a sculptor, right?"

I sip my wine and do the shrug-nod again.

"What sort of things do you do?"

"Textiles. I embroider maps of fictitious human migration patterns to create quilts."

He nods again and then the room shudders. By the time I'm

on my feet, it stops. My heart bangs against my breastbone so violently I can hear it.

"Aftershock," Dr. Wolof says. "They can go on for days."

My feet and hands go immediately cold, and my jaw starts up again. I begin breathing like a horse, big loud puffs through my nose.

"I don't want to be here," I say, turning in place. "What if the building comes down?"

"What about Leon? We should wait to get some information. I think we're pretty safe in here."

But I'm convinced that we're the only two people left in the building, that the security guard downstairs is a half-wit, shrugging and slurping his milk as we entered what was sure to become our tomb.

"I'm leaving," I say. "I'll walk to the hospital."

"But, which one? We need to find out where he is first."

"All of them. I don't care. I'm leaving." I stand and Dr. Wolof follows me, grabbing his coat and sighing. I've become his burden to bear, a big, nervous, chattering conceptual artist who he must shepherd through the worst day of her life. I don't envy his position.

We make our way back down the pitch-black stairs, temporarily blinded, feeling our way with our feet and hands.

The street is emptier than before and the security guard, the man on whose conscience our deaths would have rested, is nowhere to be seen. It's still drizzling. I have no idea where the nearest hospital is. Once I get on the street, though, I immediately start to feel better. I'm of the opinion that should something big like a telephone pole or a building come crashing down, I will be able to jump out of harm's way.

Dr. Wolof hands me my coat, which he's been carrying this whole time and says, "St. Francis is the closest, so we should probably start there." We head west, walking up the slick, dark sidewalk toward the hospital. Smoke is billowing from the north.

There's a yellow glow silhouetting the buildings. It reminds me of the way the setting sun looks through heavy fog, when you can see no source for the light but only the effect of its presence in its lasting, persistent radiance. We walk toward it like two people in a Renaissance painting.

Leon was just shy of forty when I started college. He was a bachelor. Not one of those rogues who couldn't settle down, but a man accustomed to the life of a shy, smart academic for whom the trappings of mating—dancing, wit, an interest in wine and food and music—held no allure. I was twenty, liberated by my newfound freedom, by the absence of my mother's watchful Seventh-Day Adventist eye, and by a youthful swagger that allowed me to call myself an artist and make shocking, naïve comments about sex to much older men.

I spent a lot of time in Leon's office the first semester of my junior year. At first, we leaned toward one another while he helped me understand some simple physical property like Heisenberg's Uncertainty Principle, which I memorized—*the more precisely the position is determined, the less precisely the momentum is known*—but never truly understood. I was his worst student, a flaky art major struggling to fulfill a university requirement, just the sort of student professors complain about at cocktail parties, a student with no real interest or enthusiasm for the subject. He disapproved of my carelessness with facts.

But he was magnetized by the ways in which I was careless with myself, brushing up against him and holding his gaze. All of which made me an easy target for his experimentation with some new self he was creating. I was like human training wheels, helping to steady his clumsy flirting and awkward passes.

We went on our first date shortly after the midterm, on which I scored a 68—a Yugoslavian film and Chinese food three towns over, where we were unlikely to run into any of his colleagues. If I were on that same date today, I would be nervous, eager to make a good impression. I might drink too much wine or chirp along endlessly about my art. But at the time I was drunk with my sense of myself as attractive, thrilled to be in the company of an older man who thought me so, and who I mistakenly assumed was in the possession of a long and illustrious romantic past. And because of this, our mutual surprise and intoxication with ourselves, we started sleeping together, bolstering these exhilarating new self-images we were attempting.

I moved into his rickety old redwood house the June I graduated, and shortly after, he began to take me out in public within the vicinity of the university. Shortly after that, to department functions, where I was introduced as his girlfriend and where I first started to lose confidence in my charms.

St. Francis Memorial Hospital is as loud and clamorous as a television hospital. Bloodied people on metal gurneys in the hallway chat with one another, happy to be the ones who can wait. Nurses rush around, stethoscopes bouncing against their breasts as they trot. Dr. Wolof approaches the front desk, where other anxious people are leaning, demanding answers. The computers are down. There is no complete list of patients. They've had over a hundred admitted since the earthquake, many of them for serious injuries. They tell us, the whole group of us, to calm down, to have a seat, to wait until they know more.

"We're looking for a missing person," Dr. Wolof says when he manages to catch a nurse as she moves past him behind the counter. "We just want to know if he's here."

"Call the number," she says, nodding in the direction of a handmade sign taped to the wall listing the same emergency number Dr. Wolof called back at his apartment. Technically, we're still on hold with that number; its canned music still filling the stillness of Dr. Wolof's living room.

"This was a bad idea," he says to me as we walk away from the counter, back through the crowded waiting room. "We should have stayed at my place; we can't possibly check the hospitals this way."

"He's not here, anyway," I say, taking Dr. Wolof's hand and leading him through the throng and back out to the wet sidewalk.

We walk down the block and stop at an idling car with the sound of the radio news blaring. There are four men sitting inside and a small group of other people gathered around, leaning into the windows to hear better. The newscaster is telling us the electricity is out in over half a million homes. A helicopter *thrut, thrut, thruts* over us and on cue, and we all look up, watching it pass. The news goes on to tell us about traffic jams, hospital reports on the numbers of injured, the buildings that have already collapsed, fires. This earthquake is smaller than 1906 but bigger than Loma Prieta. The President has already declared a state of emergency. We squint to picture the damage. We hear of off-ramps crumbling, and we picture ourselves exiting at that very off-ramp, our cars falling in a tumble of concrete and rebar. But soon I grow impatient. They have nothing new to tell us and simply keep reporting what we already know in an endless loop of confusion and calamity.

I watch Dr. Wolof as he cocks his head toward the radio and realize this was a stupid idea. He was right; we should've waited in the apartment for the emergency number to pick up. I can't remember why I was so scared, so completely convinced of our peril, but now I want to go back there. I don't want to go to another hospital like St. Francis, filled with the anxious stink of trauma. I want to take my chances in an empty apartment building, serenaded by tinny pop rock. I want to finish my wine while Dr. Wolof takes care of me.

I grab his arm again, and when he turns to me, I say, "Can I call you Paul?"

He looks at me surprised; he hadn't realized I'd been calling him anything else. "Of course."

"Let's go back to your place, Paul," I say. It sounds like a proposition, but I don't linger long enough to get his response. I just start walking. He, of course, comes along.

We zigzag back up and over Nob Hill. We see an apart-ment building down on one knee, lopsided and sad looking. The entrance to the building has disappeared under the splintered wood and crumbled stucco. I steer us away from it, heading left another block and then straight ahead, down a stairway. We veer north toward the ink-black bay and then east, where Oakland glows dimly in the night. Our route reminds me of one of my quilts, meandering and illogical, what one critic called "whimsical." Paul follows me, resigned to my wanderings. My route will take us twice as long, but it's helping me. All this walking in the cool, damp night is helping me to forget the sight of Leon and his inert arm emerging from under the chandelier.

When we arrive back at Paul's apartment building, my watch says it's eleven fifteen, less than four hours since the earthquake. The city is quieter now. Although sirens are still constant, they're distant. Paul's block feels like one of those futuristic disaster movies, deserted and dark. It's the *Planet of the Apes* set I was hoping for. We stop outside the entrance and look at one another. We listen and watch, taking it in like archeologists.

"Look," I say, pointing to where opaque brown water and then a panicky, flopping fish have bubbled out of the gutter.

"What happened to Leon?" he asks, ignoring me, and the fish.

I look at him, straight into his worried brown eyes, and open my mouth like I'm gasping for air. My mind scrabbles against the moment, straining to find purchase, a starting place from which I can look back on this night with a good, clear view.

Paul blinks, waiting. I could kiss him, I think.

I'm terrified again, dizzy with the awful suspicion that I've gotten it all wrong, that the chandelier never fell on him, that Leon ran away from me just in time to save himself. Or even before. "I was trying to understand it. I was trying to understand your little-known universe. But—" I'm interrupted by a great groaning and snapping across the street.

We turn and look as a building, home to a real estate office specializing in buildings of its kind, falls in on itself as if it's being sucked down by some enormous underground mouth. A cloud of dust lifts and then rumbles towards us, billowing into the wet night. I can see Paul in my periphery. "Rosie!" he says sharply as if he's trying to wake me up. And then the cloud reaches us, a blast of warm grit and chunks of cement the size of marbles, and he's swallowed up. He disappears but continues to say my name. His disembodied voice repeats itself like a ghost, and I'm tempted to find him, to grasp his hand. Instead, I close my watering eyes and cover my face until the pelting stops and then I begin to run, first north and then west, zigzagging my way through the damaged city, past abandoned cars and confused dogs, and shop windows containing tangles of fallen mannequins. There is no one else here but me, and if I keep running, I might make it to the redwood house on the side of the ravine, and find Leon where I left him.

HALO

MY MOTHER WENT SORT of crazy when she heard about my accident. It was seven in the evening in California when the call came. She didn't cry or shout or do anything that might make a good scene in a movie. Instead, after calmly making the plane reservations, she called almost everyone in her contacts and told them what had happened. This was how many of my distant high school friends, people I hadn't spoken to in years, found out I was in a coma in Idaho.

Lenny swerved to avoid a moose. I knew this made the story instantly more exotic to listeners in other states, and I learned to start with it. The car rolled, over and over, into the Idaho woods before coming to rest at the bottom of a ravine. I suppose there was screaming. Actually, I pictured it more like moaning, or a long, confused sigh. Not from me though, I had already been launched out of the car and come to rest thirty feet from the road, lying unconscious with one leg crossed primly over the other on a bed of forest mulch. I imagine there was a profound and beautiful silence when the car finally stopped. I imagine them, my new friends Lenny and April, lying stunned, looking through the cracked windshield and glittering Aspen leaves into the lavender afternoon sky.

I suppose they checked themselves, taking a mental and then

physical inventory of their bodies, terrified of what they might find. Once they realized they were miraculously unscathed, I supposed they noticed I was missing. Then they saw the shattered rear window. This was where the everyday near-disaster became the stuff of nightmares, the realization of all those fleeting, morbid thoughts. This was where it took on the slow-motion haze of the real thing. I imagine their stomachs roiled with dread.

There were sirens, speeding ambulances, lights flashing like crazy. Specialists were called off their ranches, brought in from Boise. I was mercifully aware of nothing, although when I think about it now, I feel as if I can remember a fizzing sensation at the base of my neck, right where the spine had bent and cracked.

I did wake up at one point, just long enough—a few seconds maybe—for me to realize something was terribly wrong. I didn't notice at the time that I couldn't move, only that I was intensely sleepy, unable, even with my full effort, to keep my eyes open. And then I drifted back into a coma that lasted six days.

This was about the time my mother started her delirious telephone tree in my hometown, a place I moved to Idaho to get away from, a Northern California hamlet where tract housing grew like fungus and malls projected fake evening skies onto their ceilings.

Two months later, I was in Denver at the spinal injury unit being rehabilitated. I'd long since sent my mother home, having decided it was better for my recovery to be lonely than irritated, and I got a call from Justin Findley. He'd waited ten years. If I had better use of my arms at the time, I would have dropped the phone. Instead, an orderly kindly tucked the earbuds into my ears as I spluttered out confused pleasantries and then somehow found myself agreeing to let him visit. When I hung up, the orderly removed the buds looking pleased to assist in my social re-acclimation.

The halo weighed about seven pounds. It attached to my skull via screws in four places, two on the forehead, two in the back. Four metal rods connected the metal ring encircling my head to the body harness, which fit over my shoulders like football padding and strapped around the chest. Most patients wear it anywhere from three to twelve months; my doctors made no guesses and no promises. The halo rendered me completely immobile from the shoulders up. No shrugging, no nodding, no turning to look. It prevented me from lying down completely, and it wasn't supposed to get wet. Like many cures, it was a cruel remedy, a pinching, constricting, humiliating savior.

There was a key attached to my chest. It unlocked the halo in case of an emergency, so that if I happened to have a heart attack or fall into a deep body of water, someone could uncage me to save my life. Removing the halo early posed a risk of severing my spinal cord, finally rendering me a real and forever quadriplegic.

I had two dreams. One in which I unlocked the halo myself and slid clear of it gracefully, feeling light and relieved, like a fish freed from a net. And one in which I failed to convince a stranger not to remove it. I begged and cried, trying to explain, but he couldn't hear me, and I knew once it was off, I would never move again. I woke up from that dream panting and disoriented, strangely glad to find myself locked in my halo.

There was one nurse I got along with. I liked her at first because she offered to read aloud to me and wasn't offended when I said I would rather watch Oprah. She also didn't make me do hateful things like act chipper. Her name was Siobhan, and she let me feel sorry for myself.

There was so much time in the hospital. All twenty-four hours in each day greedily stretched out their minutes, like a child who saves her candy to have some left when the others are finished. I went to physical therapy. I ate. I bathed, sometimes. I watched

Oprah and sitcoms and late-night talk shows. I read get-well cards from my friends and colleagues, talked to my mother on the phone. And I felt sorry for myself. It's so easy to do when you're twenty-eight, and you can't brush your own teeth and you're in Denver, where you don't live, and your neck is broken. It becomes like breathing, feeling sorry for yourself.

In the hospital, despite the teetering steps I was starting to take and the shaky way I could lift my hand to my mouth, they wouldn't just come out and say that I would walk normally again. Instead, they brightly uttered the obvious, "You're making progress every day," and expected me to be satisfied. But I'm impatient by nature, and I was bored with being disabled, and I just wanted a straight answer. Something to look forward to, even if it didn't pan out.

There were people much, much worse off than me. There was a rodeo cowboy who would never move or breathe on his own again. To change the channel on the television, he had to allow a machine to fill his lungs and then waste an entire breath wheezing out a request for someone to switch the station. He couldn't even cry properly because his mechanical lung didn't work quickly enough. He should have made me feel grateful, but it doesn't work that way. Someone else's greater tragedy did not diminish the size of my own.

What Justin Findley had lost in hair, he had somehow managed to gain in good looks. My lack of visitors and the screws in my skull had allowed me to forgo vanity until that moment —my looks being the least of what I might lose. His face, though, made me wince, and I was acutely aware of my own dry lips and greasy hair. For a horrible second, as he stood there in my doorway, I thought I was going to cry.

"Can you turn that off for me?" I said, as he walked in, "I

watch *Oprah* with Siobhan, one of the nurses, but I can't stand *Geraldo.* She got a call and left it on. He's awful, but anyway, hi." I was propped up, wearing sweatpants and a size forty-eight T-shirt stretched out at the neck to allow for my halo.

"Hi," Justin said. He was holding a bouquet of flowers, one of the overpriced clumps of carnations from the gift shop in the lobby. He held them out to me, and if I could have shrugged, I would have. He fumbled around awkwardly half looking for a vase, and then laid the bouquet across a chair.

"So," he said.

"So," I said.

"How have you been?"

"For the last ten years? I've been mostly good, I guess. I broke my neck. That hasn't been so good. How have you been?"

"You look amazingly great," Justin said in response. "I mean really. I thought you'd be all wrecked, but you look great."

"No scratches at least. You know how I feel about blood. I would have hated a lot of blood."

"I guess you're lucky then," he said.

"If these are my blessings, I'm pretty fucked," I said.

"No, no, I didn't mean you really are lucky. It was a joke."

"I know. I got it."

We were silent while he took in the room, tugged gently at the bottom of my blanket. I had a single room, painted in soft pink with cabbage rose wallpaper trim around the top. Sixty-seven cabbage roses, to be exact, every third one with a stem and three leaves.

"So, Justin, what in the hell are you doing here? Last time I saw you, you were standing me up outside Planned Parenthood. You're the only person in the world, besides Hitler, who I say I hate." I tried to say this in a friendly way.

He grimaced and then knitted his eyebrows. "I just can't believe this happened to you. I called once when you were in surgery and spoke to your mother. She was kind of rude to me. I don't blame her; she probably didn't tell you I called."

"My mother doesn't even know about the abortion. There's no reason for her to be rude."

"Well, she knows something. She knows you hate me."

"Maybe," I said. He was giving my mother powers of perception I doubted she possessed.

"I just can't believe this happened. Brian Newsom called me. Do you remember him? The year behind us. Ran track. He's the one who told me. It really freaked me out."

There was something horrifying about people you didn't even speak to in high school chatting about your medical condition over the phone. I had no idea who Brian Newsom was—no doubt one of the many anonymous brown-haired boys who spent their youths terrorizing the girls of suburbia.

"This is going to sound stupid," Justin continued, "but I sort of thought that I was the worst thing that would ever happen to you. I comforted myself with the idea that nothing that bad would ever happen to you again. Like me being an asshole was some sort of insurance."

"I had hoped that at one point too. Alas." I remembered the day Justin had gotten his driver's license. He drove so fast up and over the hills to the beach that the tires screeched on the turns. I clutched at the strap over the window and begged for him to slow down. "Trust me," he'd said, and I remembered making the deliberate decision to do so, deciding that being afraid got me nowhere and that if he said so, I would trust him, believing in a protection that didn't exist.

"No. Of course it wasn't," he said.

"So, you've come to apologize for ruining my life ten years late?"

"Sort of. I wanted you to know that I think about you. That it seemed like I walked away, but that I didn't completely. I think about you all the time."

I felt myself getting sleepy. My jaw ached. "That's nice," I said, yawning. I wasn't being snide. I just plain didn't have the energy to adjust my worldview. I didn't want Justin to apologize or make up, or try to explain. I didn't want him to reappear as someone other than a terrified and inconsiderate eighteen-year-old boy. What happened between us was just a fact of my life: I'm five-feet-six, I teach history, my birthday is in June, and three days after I turned eighteen, my boyfriend took me to get an abortion, said he'd be back to pick me up, and then disappeared from my life for good.

"I think I need to take a nap now," I added. Morphine was like that sometimes. Sleep was an edge I could fall right off of.

My physical therapist's name was Kahlil, and he wore his hair in a Jheri-curl, glistening with oil through his hair net. His shoulders were as round and big as my head and he clearly took his motivational skills from high school football. As I stumbled toward him, my arms hooked over the parallel bars on either side of me, he'd crouch down like a lineman and cheer me on. "Come on girl, you got it, take that step, that's it, come on, come on, come on." My goals were two-fold: To hold myself up, halo and all, and to make my feet step one in front of the other instead of flipping out in random directions. Sometimes it felt like spoon bending, and I would stare down an errant limb, forcing it with sheer concentration to set down where I intended. It made me feel as if I had never done anything hard in my life, and it made me a very difficult person to get along with.

At the end of each session, Kahlil would massage my limbs, and even though it sent currents like electric shocks through my extremities, it was by far the best part. He would quit his litany of team-building encouragements and talk to me about the patients he had worked with, about people so terribly motionless he concentrated only on their lips, on helping them to talk without the use of neck muscles.

"That's why you're my favorite," he would say, rubbing one of my tiny, folded up hands with his huge fingers, "Because someday you're going to run a fucking marathon."

There were days when all I wanted to do was curl my limp body against the massive expanse of his chest, when thinking about him made me want to weep with gratitude.

When the school year started again, I got an envelope of cards from my students. All my beautiful teenagers with their lousy spelling and their flair for drama. "We miss you!" they wrote. "Get well soon!" I would be the favorite teacher when I returned. No one could ever sass me again. I pictured myself hobbling back and forth in front of them on my cane, lecturing about the Civil War, and felt a tremendous urge to be among them. No matter what happens in your own life, it is nothing compared to the day-to-day existence of a sixteen-year-old.

Justin brought me a book the next time he visited. It felt as if it had been weeks, but it could have only been days. I had a terrible sense of time. He showed up sometime in the afternoon, just as the light was getting gloomy, and set the book down on the rolling table across my lap. It was science fiction, something that took place on another planet and involved a lot of technology. A boy book.

"I'll ask Siobhan to read it to me," I said. "Thanks."

"Shit. That was dumb. I didn't think about holding the book."

"It's a perfect gift, really. I have a lot of hours to kill, and turning pages is good practice." I twitched my hands, folded like an arthritic's, to show him what I meant.

"So, are you keeping yourself busy in here?" he asked, sitting down in my vinyl visitor's chair.

I clumsily nudged the button on my bed to move myself into a more upright position. "I hobble around trying to teach my body how to recognize walking again. I watch TV. I complain. It's boring. What do you do all day?"

I looked at him, this boy I knew so well in high school and

tried to guess what he had turned into. Real estate agent? Car salesman? If I met this man now, would I even like him?

"I own a chain of juice bars." This was something I hadn't imagined. When I failed to respond, he continued. "It's all about an upbeat, healthy lifestyle where you can still have delicious food, you know, not deprive yourself, but feel good about what you're putting into your body."

"Sounds. . ." I could not think of how it sounded. "Cool," I said.

He laughed, sort of. "I just believe in what I do. You became a teacher?"

"Yeah. Eleventh-grade American history."

"No shit. What's it like being on the other side?"

"It's exactly like it was as a student, only I'm a grown-up, and I know more, and I don't make out in the halls anymore." I remembered exactly what I wore the last day I saw him. A red sweater and jean shorts. My hair was long then, blonder.

"Did we make out in the halls?'

"Are you crazy? We practically mounted each other. God. I can't believe you don't remember that." My voice sounded squeaky. I had made the classic mistake of the uncool: showing emotion.

"I have a bad memory. I really don't think about high school very much."

I licked my chapped lips, feeling little bits of jagged skin against my tongue. "Do you remember the night I got pregnant?"

He looked away quickly, toward the door. "The night? I don't know if I ever knew the specific night it happened. It must have been around May or something, right?"

"April. We watched *Requiem for a Dream* and ate pizza. Your parents were in Carmel."

He rubbed a hand across his receding hairline. "Wow. I feel like a jerk." He didn't though, I could tell. He was just caught. Embarrassed, maybe.

"You were a jerk, Justin. You were an awful, horrible jerk. Now, I don't know. I have no idea what you are now."

Something pinged in the hallway, and an orderly came in with my dinner tray. A shriveled little pork chop cut into bite-sized pieces with a side of gray string beans and a plastic bowl of applesauce.

"I should go," Justin said, standing up and folding his jacket over his arm. "I'm meeting my girlfriend for dinner." He smiled guiltily at me, and I was momentarily stunned. I assumed he'd been flirting, checking me out in the manner of old boyfriends, and it dawned on me sharply that he most definitely wasn't. I'd forgotten for a moment that I was caged and infirm, that my XXXL T-shirt was stained and that I was someone nobody would flirt with.

"Okay," I said. "Have a good time."

Then he walked over to the head of my bed and kissed me on the cheek. That's one of the problems with being partially paralyzed. You can't sock people; you can't even turn away.

After he left, I finished everything on my tray. I ate angrily, as if I were somehow getting revenge.

Three months after my accident, I was released from the hospital. We had cupcakes in the lounge; the nurses played the Macarena, and anyone who could move, danced. It's not often that people leave this ward on their own two feet. They wouldn't say it, but I knew I was some sort of miracle.

I told my mother not to come until four. I had an appointment in the morning with my social worker. He was going to teach me how to live with my halo in the outside world for the next two months until it came off. He wanted to go over how to wash my hair (it would take another person), how to sleep in a bed that didn't go up and down, and how to manage the curious stares and rude questions from strangers. I wasn't worried about that part. People had been examining and prodding and wiping me for months. Strangers could stare at me for the rest of my life as long as I could get up and walk away.

At noon, while I was fumbling with the lock on my suitcase and getting ready to join the party in the lounge, Justin came back.

"Going somewhere?" He stood in the doorway with a coat slung over his shoulder like he was starring in a cologne commercial. He held a tall paper cup that said Groovy Juice.

"I get to go home. Well, not home, but to a crappy rented apartment a few miles away. I have to come back every other day for physical therapy. And I have to keep seeing my doctor."

"Well, congratulations. That's great. It must mean you're going to get better."

"I am better," I answered too quickly, running over the end of his sentence.

"I brought you this." He held the cup up and then set it down on the nightstand. "It's an Immune Berry Blaster." The cup sweated.

"Thanks."

"When do you get the thingamajig off?"

"It's called a halo; I get it off in two or three months. Can you get this? I'm not the world's most coordinated person yet."

"Sure," he said, lunging across the room. "Sure, sure." He snapped the lock in place and set the bag on the floor for me. When the task was accomplished, we looked at each other. "I want to tell you something," he said.

I prepared myself for another apology.

"My girlfriend is pregnant." He nodded when he spoke, as if he were agreeing with himself. "I just found out. Right after my last visit. We're having it."

I lowered myself into the sitting position on the edge of the bed. He was looking down, just like a sheepish child dragging a toe in the dirt.

"When's it due?"

"Middle of February. We're getting married, but she wants to wait. She doesn't want to look fat on her wedding day, I guess."

"I can't say that I blame her. Are you glad?"

"Yeah, I am. I'm freaked, but I'm happy."

"Freaked but happy. Yeah," I said, "me too." Justin looked at me, confused, and I could tell how neatly he was able to attribute our misunderstandings to my illness, my strangeness, some sort of deficiency I had acquired in the last ten years.

"I'm glad I came to visit you. I don't know if it accomplished anything, but I'm glad to see you," he said.

"Uh huh," I said.

"You're going to be fine. Shitty stuff happens to you, but you're always fine in the end."

"I guess. But I don't want to be the poster child for resilience. I want to be fine in the beginning, not just the end."

"That's not what I meant. I just meant—it's a good thing how you are." He stepped across the room so that he was standing over me. "I want you to know I'm not a bad person."

"It shouldn't matter what I think."

"I told you about the baby because I want you to know that this time I'm doing the right thing."

My head throbbed at the temples where the screws bit into my skin. "I'm not the judge of what the right thing is. Just because shitty stuff happens to me doesn't mean I'm a saint. But you're off the hook if that's what you want. You've been off the hook for a long time."

Justin shifted his weight. "You think I don't know you, but I do. I still know you. I know you're nicer than you pretend to be."

I opened my mouth to respond, but Siobhan ducked her head in and yelled at me for missing my own party. The sounds of pop music floated through the open door.

"Don't say anything," Justin said. "Just let me tell you that. I'm going to leave believing this was good." He leaned over and gave me and my halo an awkward embrace. The key at my chest clunked against its lock, and I grabbed at it to keep it still.

When he was gone, I stood up to make my way down to the

party. With a cane for support I could now make my feet land where I wanted, and I enjoyed the three-beat rhythm of my steps on the glossy linoleum. When I reached the lounge, I stood in the doorway for a moment watching people sway and bounce to an old Michael Jackson song. They were oblivious of me, laughing and talking and moving their broken bodies as best as they could. It was a party only we could understand, a tableau of awkward, effortful joy. Then Khalil, who'd been dancing with Robbie and her wheelchair, saw me and held out a massive hand and I stumbled toward it, ready.

MY MOTHER'S BOYFRIENDS

WE HAVE TO STAY with Carl because our mom's going to the coast for the weekend to learn how to spin wool, and our dad's down south somewhere visiting Shoshonna's family.

We find this out on Friday when we get home from school, and before we can start, our mother says, "Don't start. He'll take you swimming. It'll be fun."

We've never been inside Carl's trailer before, although we sometimes sit outside in the idling car while our mom runs in to drop something off or pick something up.

When we get there, Carl is up on a ladder attaching a basketball hoop to the top edge of his trailer. He waves at us and grins and Benny waves back, staring.

Carl is long and skinny with an empty space in his jeans where his butt should be. He's wearing an embroidered Mexican shirt with a big rip in one armpit. Our mom says, "Oh, Jesus," when she sees him, but she's smiling.

He helps us carry our bags into the trailer, then our mom looks at her watch and slaps her thighs and says she'd better get going.

"Thank you for this," she says, standing on her tiptoes to give Carl a kiss. "I know it's strange for you," she says, as if we're not standing right there, looking up at them.

We all go outside to watch her leave. She'll be back on Sunday to pick us up and by then she'll know how to spin wool into yarn, and we'll be empty from missing her.

Carl looks at us and lights a cigarette. "What now?" he asks, but we're as lost as he is, and so we just shrug, afraid to ask for anything, afraid to move really.

"What do you guys usually do on Friday afternoons?"

I try to think about this, to answer truthfully, but I can't remember. Go to our rooms? Play? Friday afternoons are no different from any other day. What we do mostly is wish we were doing something else—swimming or going for ice cream. "I'm not always with Benny," I want to tell him because it occurs to me that he might not understand that I'm ten and Benny's only five and I have a life of my own.

But Benny's standing right next to me with his fingers hooked absentmindedly through one of my belt loops.

I say, "I don't know. Play."

Benny twists around, taking in the trailer and the flattened dirt around it with his mouth hanging open a little bit. He says, "I've been wanting to learn to play cards," which seems weird and off the subject and plus, he can barely read.

I smile at Carl in a way I think shows that I know Benny's being silly, like a five-year-old. But Carl says, "I'm the best teacher you're going to find."

We go inside and sit around the Formica table in what Carl calls "the breakfast nook" but what is, we will come to under-stand, the all-meal nook as well as our bed. The table lifts and flips revealing a narrow mattress underneath. We sleep surrounded by the cushioned backs of the breakfast nook benches.

We play Go Fish and Joker, which is just like Old Maid, only the Joker is the one you don't want to get. Carl opens a bag of chips and Benny looks at me with eyebrows raised before he takes any. Our mother would have something to say about this. She thinks anything good is junk food, but she's better than Shoshonna, at least, with her wooden bowls and her kale and her brewer's yeast on popcorn.

After we get bored with cards, we sit around at the table listening to a baseball game on Carl's little radio. He doesn't have a TV, so we sit there, staring at the swirling patterns on the tabletop, just listening. Carl yells sometimes, slaps the table, but Benny and I are silent.

Before Carl there was Byron, the veterinarian. Our mom used to cut his hair outside, letting the strands fall into the dirt near the horse barn. Byron brought us buckets of strawberries and gave our mother jugs of beer he made in his basement. Once, after Benny rode his Big Wheel into the road and down along the ditch for nearly a half-mile, Byron picked him up and spanked him. Our mother, who must have seen this through the kitchen window, came running out, a blur of long brown hair and cut-offs and grabbed Byron's arm.

"What the fuck do you think you're doing?"

"I caught him riding in the road, Sandy," Byron said, but even I could tell he knew he'd made a mistake. There was no explanation in the world that was going to save him in our mother's eyes.

After Byron left, our mom pulled Benny into the house by his arm. In the kitchen she swung him into a chair and pointed her finger at him. "You," she said, "Don't do that." She left him crying and went into the living room where she sat on the couch smoking a joint. She looked at nothing, just the smoky air in front of her. I leaned against the door jamb watching her, wanting her to turn and see me, but also not wanting it.

Carl takes us to Negri's for dinner, and we get to sit at the bar and order Shirley Temples. We split a chicken-in-a-basket and first, Benny gets the minestrone and I get the antipasto, little rolls of salami and perfect squares of cheese that remind me of doll food, small and manageable. Carl orders a Jack and Coke and his own basket of chicken.

Another baseball game is on, and Carl turns toward it, yelling at the screen and talking with the other men at the bar. I recognize some of them but don't know their names except for Mr. Panazera from Panazera's Market. When I look at him, I smell the freezers and the cold stale ice that has permeated the air of his store.

The light in the bar is mostly red. The area where the tables are, over by the stage, is dark, and it's only the men, lined up against the bar with their worn-out shirts and feed caps, who are illuminated. I can see their faces reflected in the golden mirrors behind the bar, and they're all looking the same way, talking to each other without turning their faces from the TV screen. Except for Carl, they're all drinking from tall brown bottles of beer and then occasionally tilting tiny shot glasses into their slack, pouchy faces.

Benny eats three pieces of chicken and then feels sick. His lips are greasy, and he pouts and holds his stomach. When he tells me he's going to throw up, I tap the back of Carl's shoulder and tell him Benny needs to throw up.

Carl looks at me over his shoulder, then he looks at Benny.

"So, take him to the girl's bathroom; I can't stand puke. I swear. If I have to take him to puke, I'm going to puke too." He knocks his knuckles against the bar and jerks his chin at the bartender in a way I know means bring me another Jack and Coke.

I take Benny's arm and slide him off the red barstool, but he's whining now. He doesn't want to go to the girl's bathroom, and he's pulling against my arm, getting worked up about it. I'm about to force him with me into the bathroom, when he leans over and throws up all over the floor in front of the bar.

There's a gag and then a roaring sound and for a moment all the men at the bar swivel and watch as Benny leans over, coughing and spitting, long strands of throw up hanging from his lips.

"Fuck," Carl says.

The bartender leans over and hands me a wad of napkins, and as soon as Benny straightens up, looking scared and surprised, I wipe his face with one of them, folding it over as I've seen our mother do.

The men are still watching us but only the bartender has made a move. Benny stands there in front of his puddle of throw-up and starts to cry. The bartender says, "I'll get a mop. Pat the kid on the back, Carl. Jesus Christ."

Carl slides off his stool looking at the puddle like it might jump at him and picks up Benny like a baby, legs wrapped around his waist, arms around his neck. Benny puts his face on Carl's shoulder and cries harder.

"It's all right, Buddy," Carl says. "I can't tell you how many times I've done the same thing in this bar." He looks up at the men and adds, "I usually make it to the head, but hey."

Before her pottery class and before she wanted to learn how to spin wool into yarn, our mother took a film class at the junior college. Her teacher was Manny Diaz, and he lived in a development called The Ranches, a place of sloping sidewalks and perfect yellow houses. A place I loved for its regularness, each house a mirror image of its neighbor in alternating pastels, each house with a green, green patch of grass and a picture window through which we could see the lush, massive Christmas trees of the residents.

We went there only once, for Christmas Eve. Manny cooked us French food, hunks of beef and noodles in a creamy sauce. It was like nothing I'd ever eaten, and I felt that if I stopped eating, nothing that tasted so good would ever come my way again.

Benny was only two then, and my mom brought him bags of carrots and a peanut butter and honey sandwich on crumbly wheat bread. She ripped little bite sized pieces of it off for him, but she kept her eyes on Manny, who watched her across the table all night, smiling so that his eyes crinkled at the corners. They thought they were hiding something, that because they hardly spoke, I couldn't tell what was going on.

After dinner, we hung the stockings our mother made for us the year before: long, red corduroy with green trim. Our names were written in glitter down the length, and she even had one for Manny, although his was plain, no glitter. We got to open one present on Christmas Eve, and our mother left it for us in the branches of the tree so that we knew which one it was, a small something that kept us from going into a frenzy over the mounds of wrapped gifts waiting until the next morning.

That year, my Christmas Eve gift was a small pot of lip gloss that smelled strawberryish and had tiny sparkles in it, so tiny you had to move it around in the light to see them. I went into the bathroom to put it on, dipping my finger into the sticky gloss and tightening my lips. I smeared it over my bottom lip and then rubbed them together, making smacking sounds.

When I returned to the living room, Manny and my mom made such a big deal out of it I had to wipe it off. I dragged my arm across my lips, feeling the moist smear of lip gloss slide off onto my hand.

"Sweetie," my mother said, "you looked so good. Why'd you do that?"

I shrugged, unable to explain why being noticed like that made me feel like crying.

That night Benny and I had to sleep in the same bed in the back room of Manny's house. There were movie posters all over the walls and gray film canisters lined up like books on the shelves. Benny squirmed next to me sighing and holding his Snuffleupagus in the darkness above his head, moving its legs back and forth, back and forth. Tomorrow, he would forget all about this toy and it would be lost in the mounds of action figures and paint sets and maybe even, what he really wanted most, a real bike with two wheels.

I stayed awake long after Benny's breathing became light and regular, staring into the gloom, tracing the movie posters with my eyes. I could hear my mom and Manny down the hall, little knocks on the wall and grunting and laughing. I lay in the darkness for a long time listening until I realized it was probably past midnight. "It's Christmas," I whispered into the night, and then I rolled onto my side and tried to fall asleep.

We wake up long before Carl, and there's nothing for us to do. No TV, no toys. We're hungry, but we don't know how to get ourselves anything to eat in Carl's tiny kitchen. The sun shines brightly through the window, and the air in the trailer heats up and is perfectly still. Benny sweats along his hairline like a baby. When our mother knows we will be up early and she'll want to sleep in, she leaves us bowls of cereal on the kitchen table and coffee cups full of milk in the fridge. We usually carry them into the TV room and eat them there, our spoons clanging along with the cartoons.

I lie in bed and look around the tiny front room—kitchen, dining room/extra bed, and a bench under the back window. There's a metal tray of weed on the counter, shake that someone has carefully separated from the seeds. I know these words: seed, stems, bud, leaves. I know what a bong is.

Benny rolls over me and goes into the tiny bathroom. The door closes like an accordion, and it makes the noise of crushing paper. I think it'll wake up Carl for sure and even though I'm hungry, I dread this for some reason. But I wait and Benny comes out and Carl doesn't.

Saturday at Carl's is not like Saturday at the ranch. At Carl's, there are no apples to pick or horses to feed. We don't have to keep watch out for a gaggle of angry, honking geese. Outside, there's just a yard of flattened dirt and a basketball hoop on the side of the trailer and the rolling hills of California stretching out below.

I get out of bed and look through the window above the tiny sink. The dirt is already glaring, white hot. A dirty coffee cup on the counter says, "World's Greatest Grandpa." I pick it up and drop it into the aluminum sink where it bangs and rattles before settling, breaking the silence and leaving my heart pounding a little.

A few minutes later, Carl comes out of the back bedroom scratching the side of his face.

"Early risers," he says, and then he starts making coffee.

Benny and I sit on the edge of the bed watching, still afraid to ask for anything. We watch as he makes a single cup of coffee and lights a cigarette to go with it.

When he opens the door to the trailer, the bright light of the day floods in and we follow him into it and sit close by, watching as he sips from his mug and smokes and turns his face, eyes closed, towards the warmth of the sun.

After a little while, he looks at us as if he's just discovered we're there and says, "I suppose coffee and a cigarette aren't going to cut it for you two."

We go to the Coffee Cup and sit in a booth. The man behind the counter knows us and when he asks where our mom is, I whisper, "the coast." He nods and places three plastic menus in front of us.

Both Benny and I already know what we want. Pancakes and orange juice and bacon. Carl just orders another cup of coffee, but when our plates come, he leans over and takes a bite from each of ours.

"Your mom," he says, "is something special. She's not like other women. You probably know that." He tears at an empty sugar packet, not looking at us. Benny concentrates on his breakfast and nods in agreement and I think it must be nice to be only five, to not yet feel the tightening in your chest when men talk about your mother.

Christopher had perfectly feathered hair and wore tight jeans. Our mom met him at a dance, and one day he was just there in the morning, drinking coffee at our kitchen table and rubbing his forehead.

He took us to the fair, and Benny rode around on his shoulders carrying a blow-up Tasmanian Devil on a stick. The fairgrounds were hot and dry with little tufts of trampled grass sticking up.

Dust clung to the backs of our knees where it mixed with sweat in the creases. Benny and Christopher tossed dime after dime onto shiny glass dishes we would take home and pile in the bottom cupboard next to the onions.

There were days when Christopher would be asleep in our mother's bed until four in the afternoon. He spoke like this: "Man, the lines were long last night." And he left little mirrors dusted with cocaine on top of our piano.

He drank Cuba Libres, pronouncing it *Kooba*, and he stayed at our house all the time, eating and sleeping and showering there until the morning our mom got up with us to make breakfast and found the framed picture of me riding our old horse, Clover, lying on the coffee table dusted with white powder. She snatched it away so that I wouldn't see but I already had. Then she went back upstairs to her room and started yelling at Christopher.

After he left, carrying a bundle of clothes in his arms, she went into the downstairs bathroom and ran the water in the sink, and I knew she was crying. I got as much of the breakfast ready as I could, cracking the eggs into a bowl and putting the toast in the toaster.

When she came out, she made scrambled eggs and sat staring into her coffee mug as we ate them, her face puffy and tired.

Carl takes us to the river to go inner tubing, which is something we've never done and associate with kids much older than ourselves. I've seen teenagers bouncing down the river on slippery rubber rings and felt scared for them. We don't tell Carl we've never been before, that the thought of going out that far scares us. Instead, we modestly change into our swimsuits while he holds a towel around us, and then we stand next to him as he waits in line at the rental place.

The beach is crowded with people, pink-skinned girls in rainbow bikinis and tough, long-haired boys with sparse beards and fringy cut-offs. The sand is burning, and people prance across it making a big show of how much it hurts.

Benny is too small for the inner tube. If he tries to sit in it with his butt through the hole, he slips right through. If he tries to hang onto the outside, his arms get tired and the inner tube flips over. Carl tries to encourage him, yelling "There you go. That-a-boy." But my brother just gets frustrated.

We take one of the inner tubes back and Benny rides with Carl, sitting in the little puddle of water that collects in Carl's lap. Carl paddles us out, holding on to my inner tube with one arm and swiping at the river with his other. His hair's slicked back with river water, and he has a T-shirt tied around his head like a field hand.

Benny's not smiling. He's sitting in Carl's lap with his fingers dug into the sides of the inner tube. We float and sway down the river while the sun sends blinding reflections back into our faces. We pass through cold spots that send goosebumps up our legs.

I'm lying across my inner tube, keeping my body stiff so I don't slip through the hole in the middle. I can feel my scalp burning at my part, but there's nothing I can do about it; I'm holding on for dear life.

When we hit some rapids, I try to lie perfectly still to keep from bouncing out. I can see Carl and Benny ahead of me, bobbing through the little white bumps in the river, spinning a little and then, in one smooth quick motion, Benny bounces out of Carl's lap and Carl says, "Oh shit."

I hear somebody scream and realize it was me. I can see Benny. He's paddling like a dog, not crying, just gasping and looking wide-eyed in the cold, fast water. Carl slides off his inner tube and takes two strong strokes over to Benny. He grabs his slick, skinny arm in his fist and lifts him out of the water like some huge brown fish. Benny is coughing, and their inner tube rocks down the river, a shiny black ring moving quickly away from us.

As I glide past them, Carl reaches out and grabs my inner tube, swinging Benny over so he can get his arms over the sides. I feel it tip under me and then right itself and then there are three of us, clinging to the same inner tube and Benny starts laughing a little. "I swam," he says. He's grinning so that his whole face shines. "Did you see me? I swam."

Before Christopher, there were no other boyfriends; there was only our father. Our mom and dad tell two different stories about our childhood.

Once, while we helped our father scrape the tiny translucent skins of lentils off the front of the refrigerator and the walls after he exploded the pressure cooker, he described the day he left. Benny was too little, but I was almost five, and our father told me I stood on the porch, not the one we have now, but a different one, on a different house, and leaned out after him, crying.

He stopped cleaning the lentils for a moment to show me how I was. "Don't go, Daddy, don't go," he said, his mouth turned down, and his voice high in an approximation of my five-year-old self. I liked this image, but I was suspicious of it. I was too little to remember, but it didn't sound like me.

Our mother says she was the one who left, that one day she just gathered us up and stepped off that same front porch. It's mixed up in my head with the story about Benny's first sentence, which was "Make me toast," and even though I know they didn't happen on the same day, I picture my mother scooping Benny from his highchair as he demands toast and leaving out the front door, me clinging to her leg. I can see her, and I can see Benny, but I can't see myself. I know I'm there; I just don't know what I look like.

In her version, it was our father who cried. He was the one who stood on the porch, leaning out after us, begging us not to go.

"It wasn't an easy day," she says, "But it turned out okay. He let me come back for my stuff, at least. He rose to the occasion."

We are terribly sunburned, and Carl gives us ice cubes wrapped in paper towels to rub on ourselves. We sit in lawn chairs in the dirt outside Carl's trailer, waiting for our hot dogs. He leans over the hibachi poking at them with a metal fork. A neighbor's dog lies in the dirt like he lives there.

Benny tells us again about his swim in the river. He talks about fossils now, about how many fossils he could see when he went under. I think I know what he means, those bright, squirming amoebic things that sometimes appear when you close your eyes.

Tomorrow, after lunch, our mother will come. Carl has already asked us not to tell her about the inner tubes. He stopped as we meandered the aisles of Panazera's for hot dogs and buns and Eskimo pies and said, "I think your mom would just get worried if we told her about today. Why don't we just say we went swimming and tell her we had a great time."

"Yes," Benny says, guileless, but I know that he'll tell her, that he won't be able to resist the story of him swimming, of all his self-sufficient buoyancy.

The hot dogs Carl makes us are black on the outside, their skin crisp and puckered. We drown them in ketchup and eat them quickly, wanting more. We are starving and sun-drenched and sleepy.

Tonight, we will sleep together in the breakfast nook bed and dream of different things. Benny will see himself swimming; he will be able to breathe water and dive among the rocks for fossils. In his dream, he will jump from the water like a fish, gleaming for a moment in the sun before splashing back down, fearless.

I'll dream of my mother's boyfriends all at once. They'll be lined up on the front porch, not the one we have now, but a different one, on a different house, a house I don't remember seeing but that will make perfect sense in my imagination. In the dream, we'll be leaving. My mother will have Benny in her arms, and I'll be behind them holding on to the hem of her skirt. As we step off the front porch, we'll hear the boyfriends crying, and when I turn around to see their faces, I'll sense myself among them. I don't see myself exactly, but I know I'm there, waiting with the boyfriends and my father as Benny and our mother and another version of myself disappear at the end of the yard.

DANCES

WE'RE SUPPOSED TO BE asleep in the van. Instead, we're sitting up in the bed our mother fashioned on the floor, peering out between paisley curtains at three people splitting a joint. We're in the parking lot at the community center, and inside a band from the next town over is playing Country Joe and the Fish covers. It's Saturday night, and the parking lot is full. My mother's due to check on us in another five minutes. She comes every half hour, and we pretend to be asleep.

My brother is five and scanning the parking lot for people making out. Once, a couple banged right up against the blue sides of our van and started humping. My brother laughed so hard he peed the bed a little. I'm watching the open doors of the community center for our mother. I'm timing her on the new digital watch our dad gave me. Eight more minutes. It's eleven twenty-two.

The band is playing a song I recognize from our house. My brother is on his knees in his tiny white underwear playing air guitar and cracking himself up. He's bored watching for couples making out. He pulls down the front of his underpants and shakes his penis at me and then falls backwards against the pillows laughing. I hate it when he gets like this, all crazy and bored. I pull my blanket out from under him and then turn back to the window. The best thing to do is just try to ignore him. He sings "Angie" to me the way our mom sometimes does, but I keep ignoring him. Our mom is already two minutes late.

She's wearing brown cords and a flowered peasant top she's pulled down off her shoulders. When I see her framed in the light of the community center doors, I yell, "Coming!"

My brother and I dive under the covers and close our eyes. He's laughing through his nose, and I know he'll give us away.

Our mother slides the van door open as quietly as she can, but it clangs and grinds anyway. My brother sits up and says hi like he just woke up, all soft and sleepy.

"Hi, Benny baby," she says, climbing in and lying down next to us.

"Hi," I say too because I can't stand pretending to be asleep anymore.

"Angie too. Both my babies are awake." She smells like smoke and wine and sweat. I try to roll over Benny so that I can lie next to her, but he does that thing where he makes his whole body hard, nothing but edges, and I can't budge him.

"It's loud," I say.

"Is it?" our mother asks. She's distracted and doesn't notice the way the band's music thumps against the sides of the van. She reaches over and smooths my bangs back against my head. "Try to go back to sleep. I'll stay here until you do and then when you wake up it'll be morning and we'll be at home." She sits up and peers out the paisley curtains towards the community center doors. Her hair is wet around her face and stuck to the back of her neck. I want her to lie down and go to sleep with us, but I know she's looking out the window for Carl. I look at my digital watch. It's not even midnight yet. The dance doesn't end until two. I close my eyes and feel sleep pressing down on me against my will. I try to stay awake, but I can't.

My brother sweats so hard in his sleep I wake up and think he's peed the bed again. I kick the covers off. The band is playing another song I know from my mother's parties. Carl's band plays it sometimes in our basement. American woman, get away from me.

I press my cheek against the window and blow the curtain away to watch it flutter. There's a cluster of people around the community center doors. I recognize Billy from the place where my mom buys hay for the horses. Clouds of smoke boil above them like storm clouds and when one of them laughs, they all laugh, bending back and forth and screeching like birds. My brother says "ahh" in his sleep and rolls over, and then the van door slides open.

Carl's hair is down to his shoulders and wet. He recently shaved his moustache off, and he looks weird to me.

"You still up?" he says, looking at me.

"It's loud," I whisper. "I just woke up."

"Should I tell your mom you're up?" He's standing outside with the van door open. Cool night air and the crashing sounds of the dance rush in.

"Nah," I say. I just want him to go back to the dance. It wasn't so bad being awake by myself. But he climbs in and sits on the edge of our makeshift bed.

"That's a good girl. She's having too good a time to be bothered right now anyway." He takes a pack of cigarettes out of his breast pocket and shakes one out. He lights it and then touches the end of the match to his tongue to put it out. It makes a tiny sizzling sound. "Man," he says, exhaling, "your mom can dance. She just about kills me the way she can dance. I think half the men in this county are in love with her."

I put my palm flat against the window to feel its coolness. My brother groans a little and turns his face into the pillow. My mom says he's more sensitive to stuff than me, and I wonder why he's still asleep and I'm awake.

Carl holds his cigarette between his first and second fingers and uses his thumb to pick something out from under the fingernail on his other hand. "Your mom," he says. Then he stops and takes a drag of his cigarette. He turns his head and looks at me. "Lay down," he says. "You're never gonna fall back asleep sitting up like that. What time is it anyway?"

I look at my digital watch. "One-oh-seven."

He lies down so that Benny is between us, and smokes looking up at the ceiling of the van. I lie down too and look where he looks. Tiny spots of rust bloom like flowers on the roof.

"Do you like me?" Carl asks. He blows smoke in a column to the ceiling where it spreads like a mushroom cloud.

"Uh huh," I say. I close my eyes, hoping that sleep will come.

"Your mom isn't sure whether you and Benny like me. She doesn't want me to move in because she's not sure if you guys would like it." I don't say anything. I'm trying to feel heaviness in my eyelids. "Would you?"

"I guess," I say.

"You guess? Either you would or you wouldn't."

"I don't know," I say. I wonder if my mom is going to come out and check on us, or if she's sent Carl in her place.

"That means you wouldn't." He smokes for a while and then says, "I can understand it. You want your mommy all to yourself. Yeah, I can understand it."

It doesn't seem like he is talking to me, so I don't say anything. My eyes are still closed but I can feel Carl moving. I hear him kiss my brother. Then I feel his big head lower towards my face. I can see him even though my eyes are closed. When his lips touch the corner of my mouth, leaving a tiny spot of wetness, I hold my breath. His breath feels hot and gritty, and it smells like an ashtray. He keeps his face close to mine and says, "sweet dreams." Then he gets up and leaves. When the van door slides shut behind him, I open my eyes. Benny looks right at me and says, "I don't want Carl to live with us."

We're awake, lying in bed being quiet, until the dance ends. My old red sleeping bag is unzipped so that it lays over us like a blanket, and we both have Big Bird pillowcases left over from when I was little. Benny is playing with his fingers, holding them above his face and doing "Itsy Bitsy Spider" without singing.

The way everyone comes streaming out of the community center doors in long columns reminds me of blood moving through veins. I've seen it on TV; it rushes and stops, rushes and stops.

Our mother yanks open the van door and throws her purse in the back with us. I can tell by the way she doesn't even care that it hits my brother in the shoulder that she's mad.

"I thought I told you to go back to sleep," she says to us without looking.

We don't say anything, just keep lying on our backs looking at her sideways. She slams the sliding door shut and gets in the driver's seat. There's nowhere to go yet. A long line of cars is blocking the way to the exit. She sighs, and I can see her jaw throbbing.

When Carl taps on her window she gasps. "Jesus, fucking Christ!"

"Sandy," he says in a tired voice, "come on."

She rolls down the window. "Come on what, Carl?"

"Just calm down for a second. There's nothing to get mad about."

My mother points her finger at Carl, almost touching his nose. "Leave them out of this, Carl. Just leave them the fuck out of it."

Carl deflates. "Jesus, Sandy—" he starts, but my mom puts the van in gear and lurches forward. The wheels screech under us, and I roll against my brother like a barrel.

My best friend Jill's parents are Christians. I go to their house after school to drink Kool-Aid and play Lite-Brite. Jill's room is all yellow ruffles. Her mother made the curtains herself. My mother calls Jill's mother the "Great White Hope" behind her back. Maybe because she's so fat.

Once, when our mom came to pick me up, Jill's mom invited her in for lemonade and then started talking about God. She had all these little comic books with pictures of heaven in them that she wanted our mom to take home. Our mom gathered them up, made a neat little pile, and pushed them back at Jill's mom. "Sorry, Nancy. I'm just a heathen, born and bred," she said. Later, when I asked her what a heathen was, she said it's someone who's going to hell and likes it that way.

When I stay for dinner at Jill's house, we say grace and include my mom in the list of people we pray for. In my mind, I plead with God to save her from hell. She won't let me go to church with them on Sundays because she says they'll brainwash me, and I'll grow up to be a housewife, but Jill's mom taught me how to pray so I can do it by myself, quietly.

Benny and I are up hours before our mom. It's Saturday, and we watch cartoons in the living room. When she wakes up, she'll make us go outside; she'll urge us to climb trees and catch snakes and be more dangerous. "Jesus, I thought I was going to get country kids," she'll say.

Most of the time, Carl's here on Saturday mornings. He sits on the couch smoking cigarettes and watching cartoons with us while our mom makes coffee and reads the paper at the kitchen table. Carl buys Fruit Loops and keeps them in our cupboard. Benny and I aren't allowed to eat them because they're Carl's and because they're too sugary. When Benny and I sneak, we eat only five loops at a time so no one will notice they're missing.

By the time our mom gets up, we're already bored with cartoons, sitting numbly through the ones about robots. But at least Carl's not here. "You guys should be outside," she says. She's in her bathrobe and her hair is matted on one side. When she sits on the couch, she groans a little. Benny and I look at her, waiting for something. She pats the couch on either side of her, and we jump up off the floor and snuggle into her like puppies.

"Want to do something fun today?" she asks.

Benny yells, "Swimming!"

"Angie?"

"Swimming," I say, but I doubt it will be very fun. Our mom will just lie on her back with her hand over her eyes, only pretending to watch when we beg her to. At least Carl plays with us when we go to the river. We climb up his big, slick back, and he lets us jump off his shoulders.

"Ok. Swimming. But now you go outside and play while I read the paper. We'll go in the afternoon." She pats our bottoms. "Up."

Benny and I end up at Ernie and Tajali's. They rent the cottage beside the barn. My mom says their rent is cheap because of the smell from the goats. They're visiting Tajali's sister in San Francisco, so the cottage is empty.

Benny and I aren't supposed to go in there when they aren't home, but the rest of the ranch bores us, and they never lock their door. All their walls are wood, and in the corner that serves as a kitchen, the pots and pans hang from nails. Old mayonnaise and mustard jars are filled with beans and rice and powders of all different colors. It smells like dirt and tea, a little moldy. Sometimes Benny and I make mixtures from the stuff in the jars, but today we just look around, sniffing the mugs Ernie makes and looking at photographs we've looked at a million times.

Their biggest piece of furniture is an armchair carved out of a redwood trunk. It's smooth and old and polished to a deep, glowing red. On the seat are cushions Tajali made from Indian fabric. Benny calls it the hobbit chair, and when he sees me about to sit in it, he races toward me and slams his butt in the chair first so that when I sit, I sit on his lap. I press down on him, making myself heavy, and he giggles until I do it too hard, and then he whines and starts to fake cry. I press harder, and he screams at me to stop but he's just being a baby, and I know I'm not really hurting him.

It's past noon and my stomach grumbles. In Ernie's and Tajali's refrigerator, there is nothing good: plain yogurt, miso paste, some wilted vegetables on the bottom shelf. I open a box of Ak-Maks and eat them absentmindedly, watching the dust float like stars in the shaft of light coming through the skylight. It's so hot the room almost buzzes.

I look out the window at our crumbly yellow house. Last month, Carl nailed up new screens on the sun porch, so it looks a little better. I want my mom to come out and take us swimming, and I feel like if I stare hard enough, she will read my mind and come find us. My mouth is full of cracker paste, but I stuff in another Ak-Mak.

Carl's car makes a crackling sound against the dirt road that leads to our house, and as soon as I see him, I'm not hungry anymore. He pulls up in front of the porch. I take the box of Ak-Maks to the window and sit on the floor. Carl knocks on the front door of the house, which he never does. He squints over his shoulder at the cottage, but he can't see us through the window. As I watch him, I understand that we will not be going swimming.

Benny slides off the redwood chair and comes to the window. He's chewing the side of his cheek like he does. He still looks like a baby sometimes.

When our mom answers the door, she braces her hands against the door jamb and fills the doorway with her body. She's wearing shorts and a tank top, and I can see her bra straps. Her feet are bare and crossed over one another. Benny breathes loudly through his mouth.

After our mom lets Carl in the door, she pokes her head outside and looks both ways. I know she's looking for me and Benny, but I don't move. A fly buzzes and smashes itself against the window, and my heart races at the sound.

Carl is in there so long, we get bored watching the front of the yellow, crumbly house. Benny is hungry but the Ak-Maks are almost gone so I don't give him any. Instead, we go to the orchard to see if there are any good apples on the ground. The trees are old and uncared for. Knotted, gnarled trunks that look like something diseased. The weeds come up to our chests. Last Halloween, our mom had a party and made apple cider, but it tasted awful, so Carl made a beer run instead. Our house was full of witches and fairies and a man wearing nothing but a tiny piece of leather over his privates. Benny and I sat on the couch watching the grown-ups dance and eating from our big, lumpy bags of candy.

We find some small hard apples on the ground and shine them on our shirts. Benny spits on his because he thinks it makes them look extra good. We're sitting on the back steps of our house, the ones no one ever uses, when we hear something crash. I feel the vibration in my chest at the same time I hear it. It ends as quickly as it began, with a thud.

We run around the front of the house and see Carl get into his car. He looks at us for a moment, and we freeze, wonder what he's going to do to us. Carl has never yelled at us. I clutch the front of Benny's shirt to keep him from running any further. Carl looks at us and says, "Apparently, I'm not allowed to talk to you little fuckers." He gets into his car. He drives so fast out of our long driveway that rocks shoot from behind his wheels.

I drop my apple in the driveway. I'm still holding Benny's T-shirt, and he twists to get away from me and runs toward the house. I run after him, trying to make him stop. I understand that he shouldn't go into the house first. We reach our mother at the same time. She's sitting on the linoleum in the kitchen with her legs splayed out in front of her like a child. Our old black phone has been ripped off the wall, and it lies beside her, the receiver stretched away from the base. I start to cry.

"Oh, my babies. It's okay." She holds out her arms to us and we go to her and sit between her legs. Benny and I cry into her soft chest. She smells like dust and coffee.

I lift my head, "Carl," I choke out.

"He got mad at me, honey," she says. "But it's okay now." She strokes the tops of our heads, and we lift our faces towards her like flowers to the sun. "Don't worry," she says. "I'm okay."

On Sunday, our mom lets me go to church with Jill's family. As I ride with them to Sebastopol, I feel excitement rising in me like bubbles. I love Sebastopol. I love the A&W and the drugstore where we go bathing suit shopping. I love the teenagers who gather in clumps on the street laughing and flipping their hair. After church, Jill's mom is taking us to the International House of Pancakes, and I'm sure she'll let me order the chocolate chip kind with whipped cream.

Outside the church, ladies in flowered dresses and white sandals mill around smiling at each other. They all wear pantyhose and look so beautiful. When I go shopping with my mom, I try to sneak the egg-shaped packages of nylons into our cart, but it never works.

The church is made of gray bricks and one corner of the roof juts into the sky like a wing. Inside it's cool and quiet, and colored light from the stained glass falls against my lap. I'm wearing a pair of Jill's sandals, and I love the way my feet look in them.

Jill's mom sits between us and keeps looking down at me and smiling. The minister is in a long white robe, and he talks and talks about things I can't follow. At the end, there is singing, and I stand and watch the beautiful faces of the ladies. They sing with their eyes closed, smiling. Jill sings too, and I ache to know the words.

When it's time to pray, I bow my head and think about my mom. Jill's mom holds my hand. "Please God," I say. But I can't think of what to ask for. "Please help her to know the truth," I say, because it's how Jill's mom taught me to pray. My throat closes on itself, and my eyes start to sting. I squeeze my eyes shut, but it doesn't help; the sound coming from my mouth is a soft wail, and I can feel all the pretty church ladies looking at me. I look at my feet in Jill's sandals, and they blur and swim. I can't stop; I start to say "Please, please, please" over and over until Jill's mom scoops me up against her huge soft belly and leads me outside where the sunshine blinds me.

I stop crying in the car, but I ask Jill's mom to take me home. I don't want to go to the International House of Pancakes. I want to go home and see my own mom in her cut-offs and tank top. I want to play in my own room, without yellow ruffles and cookies on trays.

When Jill's mom drops me off in front of our crumbly yellow house, I try to convince her not to come in. "My mom doesn't like surprise visits," I say. It feels impetrative that she stay in the car and I refuse to get out until Jill's mom sighs and says, "Okay, honey," and lets me go into the house alone.

The house is quiet and dry, pierced by squares of light from the windows. My mom is in the kitchen reading the paper and drinking coffee. Benny is playing at his friend Shane's house, and I'm glad he's not home.

When she looks up at me, I start to cry again. Not as hard, but I can't stop the hot tears rolling from my eyes. My mouth turns down. My mother's hair is still not combed, and her smooth, tanned skin is blotchy and red. For the first time in my life, I think she looks ugly.

"I don't want to go to the dances anymore," I say. "I hate sleeping in the van." I'm about to tell her I hate Carl, but I stop. I know enough to know that it's not his fault.

My mother looks at me for a minute as if I'm a stranger. Then she pats her thigh and I go to her. I bend from the waist and bury my face in her lap. She strokes my hair and rubs circles on my back.

"Baby," she says. "I'm all danced out for now." She laughs a little.

I stand there, bent at the waist until I stop crying. My mom hooks her foot around another chair and drags it over for me. She pats the seat and asks, "How was church?"

"Okay." My eyes feel puffy and dried out.

"Did you find Jesus?"

I think for a moment about the colored light and the beautiful ladies and the singing. "Not really," I say.

"Just remember what I said about those women, Angie. They're not as happy as they appear to be."

SUDDEN FICTIONS

THIS IS HOW I started screwing the janitor. I was sitting in the computer lab. It's a tiny, windowless room on the fifth floor where graduate students go to print out papers. I go there at night and on weekends because it's empty and I can get away from my dogs. It makes me feel as if I have an office, as if the critiques I write of my students' work are meaningful pursuits. I eat muffins and put my feet up and read sections of their stories aloud to myself. *I followed him into their bedroom where my sister was sweetly laid on their bed.*

I'd mistakenly asked my students to narrate an important emotional event from their pasts, and I was reading my ninth paper about the pressures of being a high school athlete when he opened the door to empty the trash and sweep the floor.

I'd noticed him in the building before. He was on the short side, stocky in a way that I liked. He wore a big straw hat when the weather was good, and for a while, I thought he was a new graduate student. Then I noticed him pushing around a trash can on wheels.

I looked up, startled, and put my feet on the floor. I was only making more of a mess for him by having my dirty shoes on the desk like that.

"Sorry," I said. He looked at me and smiled without parting his lips. He propped the door open with his rolling trash can, and I could feel the cool air from the hall rush in. "Stuffy," I said.

"No windows," he answered. He grabbed the gray metal wastepaper basket and turned it upside down over his trash can. Then he took a plastic liner out of his pocket and shook it open with a loud snap.

"It's private in here, though. I get a lot of work done."

He looked up at me. "You don't have to explain. You're allowed in here." He tucked the plastic liner into the wastepaper basket, then he unhooked a long, cloth, push-broom from his cart and began to run it across the shiny floor.

I looked down at the story I'd been reading. It was about not winning MVP of the volleyball team. I looked up at the janitor again. "How long does it take you to do the whole building?"

"On Sundays, I just empty and sweep. Takes about two hours when I'm good."

"But you're here every day."

"Different jobs on different days. I only do the bathrooms Mondays, Wednesdays, and Fridays. You get the picture."

"I teach on those days. Beginning Fiction Writing. It's okay, I guess. Pays the bills." I smiled.

"That's what jobs do, I guess." He finished with the floor and shook his broom over the trash can. He opened the door a little wider to get his cart unwedged, and then he left the computer lab.

I turned back to the drama of the awards ceremony and circled the words *pist off* in red ballpoint.

At ten, I gathered up my piles of papers and my thermal coffee mug and left to go home. I still had five stories left, but I was tired and in no mood to go on with tales of spring dance couplings and homecoming game injuries. I'd wake up early the next morning and finish them before class.

I went into the bathroom on the first floor and locked myself in a stall to pee. As I pulled down my too-tight jeans and sat, I heard the outside door open and the sound of the janitor's voice.

"Hello?" he called out.

"I'm in here," I shouted. "Just a second." The sound of my

urine hitting the toilet water echoed off the tiles. "I'll be right out." I didn't hear him leave.

Then he said, as if it were perfectly normal for him to be standing there listening to me pee, "I'm done for the night."

"Oh?" I wished he would wait for me in the hall.

"I was wondering if you were also done for the night."

"I was heading home."

"Do you want to go get coffee then?"

I flushed and opened the stall door and saw him there, leaning against the sink. "What's your name?" I asked.

"Mitchell," he said, sticking out his hand. "Yours?"

"Genevieve." I held out my unwashed hand, and he squeezed it briefly. He smelled like soil. "I have my car. Where should I meet you?" I asked, my stomach contracting like a sea anemone.

We went to Denny's on the other side of I-80 because it was late and nothing better was open. We got a booth by the window. He ordered a black coffee and a short stack of blueberry pancakes. I had herbal tea. When he got up to use the bathroom, I smoothed my eyebrows and ran lip gloss across my lips.

"You're in English?" he asked, sliding into the booth.

"Kind of. Creative Writing."

"English students are the best recyclers. Better than Romance Languages and way better than Philosophy." I watched the wrinkles at the sides of his mouth, thumbnail-sized half-moons that framed his lips like parentheses.

"Is that so? So, tell me Mitchell, how did you end up here, as the janitor, I mean."

"Custodian."

"Sorry. How'd you end up here as the custodian?"

"Moved to Davis, wasn't interested in college. I don't mind it. Pays the bills," he said, smiling at me. "And you?"

"What? In grad school? Nothing better to do, I guess. I like to write." I leaned forward on my elbows so that my face was closer to his. Our feet were barely touching under the table.

"I see," he said, smiling, and I decided right then that I would sleep with him. "What do you write?"

"Fiction," I said, leaning back against the backrest and holding his gaze. I was playing it cool.

The waitress came and set down our drinks, then she went back to the counter and brought over Mitchell's steaming pancakes. Conversation paused while he prepared them meticulously, buttering each layer and using lots of syrup.

"You French?" he asked, cutting into his food with the edge of his fork.

"No. Why?"

"Genevieve. It sounds French to me."

"Oh. Nope. My mom likes romance novels. I'm named after the heroine of the one she was reading when I was born."

"Interesting. I'm Jewish."

"Ah," I said.

"Not too many Jewish custodians around. Both my brothers are dentists. They make wads of cash."

"Your parents must be very proud of you," I said.

"Their sweet college dropout, pushing brooms for a living. But," he added, brightening a little, "I get to wear flip-flops to work, so it's worth it."

"Why'd you drop out?"

"Because eight months into my freshman year, I realized that higher education was nothing more than sitting on your ass learning about people who actually did stuff."

I prickled. I had spent the last twenty years in school. Being in school was maybe my greatest talent. I sipped my tea and concentrated on his neck, which was tanned and smooth.

He looked up at me, his mouth full of pancakes and his face full of confidence. "So, I'll never be a dentist, but at least I didn't spend four years sitting on my ass."

"I hate dentists," I said, and moved my foot slightly so that it was flush against his.

"Me too," he said, smiling.

We went to my house because it was closer, and I needed to let my dogs out. As I stood at the front door, struggling with the lock, Mitchell came up behind me and put his hands on my hips. "I like smart women," he said into my ear. I turned around in his arms and kissed him. He tasted like coffee and syrup and cigarettes, which was nice.

We opened the door, and my dogs came charging at us. They were named Tina and Turner. But for reasons I couldn't explain, I sometimes called them Mark and Lulu.

Mitchell wandered around my living room, looking at book spines and picking up framed photos of my family.

I listened my messages. I had stupidly given my cell number out to my students that year. The only message was from Joelle. She wanted to know if she was allowed to write her next story from the perspective of a parakeet.

I wrote myself a note to respond later and pressed DELETE.

"That's my sister," I said to Mitchell. "Her name's Wilhelmina. When she was born, my mother was reading a book set in Germany. We call her Willie."

"Pretty," Mitchell said, and I flinched. Willie has been crazy beautiful since the day she was born.

"She's very young. Nineteen." He set down the picture of Willie and walked over to me.

"You're prettier," he said, wrapping his arms around my waist and kissing me again. I was not prettier. Few were. I kissed him back.

"So …," he said.

"So," I said. Then I took his hand and led him into the bedroom. That was in September.

In November, my students started workshop. I made them put their desks in a circle and told them I was no longer leading class. It was up to them.

"We'll start with Joelle's story, 'Freebird.'" I sat silently, waiting for them to begin.

"I think it was really cool how this is a story told by a bird," Colin said.

"I liked it a lot," Stefani said.

"I was wondering what the cage stood for," Diego asked.

I tapped my pen and drank Diet 7UP. Then I told them to stop being so goddamned nice, and Joelle turned bright red and left the room.

On Wednesdays, Fridays, and Sundays, I'd work in the computer room while Mitchell cleaned the building. Then we'd drive back to my place in separate cars. On the first Sunday in November, he asked me if I had Thanksgiving plans.

"I noticed that Denny's offers the complete meal for twelve ninety-nine. I was thinking about it."

"I'm meeting my family in Palm Springs; we do it every year since my parents retired. You could come." He was lying on top of me, making it hard for me to breathe.

"Families don't like me. Besides, I'm trying to lose weight."

He kissed my neck. "I like your figure."

"I'll think about it," I said, rolling him off me.

"I'm sure they'd love you, if it's any help."

"Who'd love me?"

"All of them. Mom, Dad, and the two dentists."

"Oh, God. Forget it."

On Monday, Renée came to my office hours. I could tell from the big symmetrical curls in her hair that she used hot rollers every morning.

"Ms. Pinkerton," she said, "I can't participate in workshop. Everything I write is so personal. I just need to keep it special; you know?"

I was eating an egg salad sandwich, and I wiped the corners of my mouth, aware that teachers seem especially prone to gooey white stuff collecting on their lips.

"Renée, this is a fiction writing class. We tell stories. Which means we tell stories *to* someone. You have to participate in workshop."

"Then everyone will know all this personal stuff about me." She looked as if she might cry.

"Renée, what you need to do is become a better liar." I bit into my sandwich and looked at her.

"Will I get an F if I don't participate?"

"Yes," I said, "you will."

On Tuesday, I ran into Mitchell in the elevator. I was talking to my thesis advisor when Mitchell got on at the second floor. He smiled and maneuvered his rolling trash can into the corner of the elevator. He wore big black gloves and a chain that hung between his belt loop and front pocket.

"Hi, Mitchell," I said. "Do you know Professor Maybaum?"

"I don't believe we've met." He held out a gloved hand.

"Pleased to meet you," she said, holding up her briefcase and a fistful of papers to indicate she couldn't shake his hand.

The three of us stood staring up at the lit red numbers blinking above the door. I was acutely conscious of my own breathing, which sounded fast and deliberate. Mitchell put his hand on my ass right before the red five lit up and my knees buckled slightly in surprise. I did a little hop out of his reach and looked at Professor Maybaum who was staring at a spot somewhere near the middle of the door.

The elevator stopped on the fifth floor, and I held the doors open as Mitchell steered his cart out into the hall.

"Meet me in my office at two," he said to me.

"Yep," I said brightly as if we were simply confirming a meeting. I waved as the doors slid shut.

"He's the janitor?" Professor Maybaum asked.

"The custodian," I said.

"And he has an office?"

"Sort of," I said, shrugging.

At two, I knocked on the door to Mitchell's room in the basement of Dowling Hall. The ceilings hummed and gurgled with the sound of water rushing, toilets being flushed, hands being washed. The floor was concrete and dusty, and the walls were cinder block painted in an institutional yellow. I could hear Mitchell approaching the door by the jingle of his keychain.

"I thought you might want a snack," he said, handing me a beer as I crossed the threshold. His room was tiny and windowless. One wall was covered with battered old lockers. Stacked neatly on another wall were cans of cleaning stuff: Ajax, floor wax, industrial-sized jugs of window cleaner.

He motioned for me to sit on the old metal desk, and I hopped onto it awkwardly, feeling my jeans pinch in the thighs.

"You must get high working with all these chemicals," I said, motioning to his shelves. He shrugged and rolled the chair he sat on over to the desk. His head was level with my crotch, and he leaned in between my legs and kissed the seam of my pants. I laughed a puff of air out my nose and took another sip of beer.

"Let's," Mitchell said, going to work on the buttons of my jeans. I lay back, my head resting on a plastic-wrapped roll of paper towels and let him work my pants over my butt and down past my ankles.

He nuzzled my knees apart with his head. I knocked over my beer, and for the next twenty minutes I listened to it drip to the floor and fizz.

On Wednesday, Mitchell did not feel like having sex with me. I lay next to him, stymied. I wasn't quite sure what we'd do if we weren't going to have sex.

"I want you to come to Palm Springs. I've never brought anyone home for the holidays."

"I was going to try and catch up on some things over the long weekend. I really don't have the time." I ran my foot up his leg, hoping to change the subject.

"In Palm Springs, you can work by the pool."

"But Mitchell, we're just *sleeping* together. It's not as if I'm your girlfriend or anything." I kissed the hollow between his shoulder and his chest. "I mean, how would you introduce me to your parents? 'Mom, this is the girl I screw three nights a week?'"

"You're too much," Mitchell said, getting out of bed and walking naked over to the chair where his clothes were.

"You're leaving?"

"I'm not in the mood for your jokes tonight."

I sat silently while Mitchell put on his clothes. He left the bedroom still buttoning his shirt. If we were in one of my students' stories, I would whip out a machine gun, and the whole event would end in a murder-suicide. Blood would drip down the walls. But we weren't, so I listened to him go out the front door, and then I got up to make some tea. It was a good time to feel sorry for myself, abandoned in bed on a Wednesday night.

Thursday is one of Mitchell's days off. I don't know what he does on his days off, really. Maybe he cleans his own apart-ment, although I doubt he's in any mood to clean when he doesn't have to. I knew a gourmet chef once who ate nothing but Cheerios at home.

I spent my Thursday at home. I wrote an email to my mother wishing her a happy Thanksgiving. Telling her I wished I could be there but that graduate school had me swamped. I would be home for Christmas, I promised, guiltily adding X's and O's.

Then I went out to lunch with my friend Margaret in Comp Lit. She's a vegetarian, so we went to an Indian restaurant for saag paneer and samosas.

"So," I said, "did I tell you that I'm sleeping with the janitor?"

"What janitor?" She stopped with her fork perched between her plate and her mouth. Her lips were parted slightly in anticipation.

"The one who cleans Dowling. *Our* janitor."

"The one with the hat?" Margaret finished her bite and let her fork clatter on her plate. She tended toward the dramatic. "No way!"

"Do you think I'm bad?"

"I just want to know how he is in bed. God. I love a manual laborer."

"He's very sweet. But not the grunting brute you're envisioning."

She ignored me. "Oh, you're so lucky. Academics never have any muscle. Have you noticed that? I'm going to have to start dating people from the real world," she said.

"Try the Animal Husbandry department. All that feed lifting and hay baling. And we're not *dating*. We're *sleeping* together." I pointed a fork with a potato on the end at her.

She rolled her eyes and tilted her head to indicate she didn't believe me. "You're so damn lucky." Margaret drank wine with lunch. She studied French literature, so it made sense.

"I guess, but I'm going to have to end it. He thinks college is a waste of time *and* he wants me to go to meet his parents on Thanksgiving."

"Here?"

"Palm Springs. He wants me to go with him for the whole vacation."

"Are you nuts? Go!" Margaret stuck her head forward and bugged out her eyes. It was supposed to look like shock, but for a moment I thought she might be choking.

"Why in the world would I want to meet his parents?"

"Because he asked you to. Jesus, Genevieve, for a woman you sure do act like a man."

"I don't act like a man, Margaret. I'm a realist, a pragmatist."

"Well, even if true love is your nightmare, you should still go. Get out of Davis, work on a tan."

"I'll think about it, I guess. But I just know his parents are the types who expect you to dress up for dinner. I don't think I can do it, you know, the whole white-shoes-Palm-Springs-family-holiday bullshit. Besides, I do have a lot of work to do." I finished my Chardonnay.

Margaret looked hurt for a minute and then said, "Did I tell you I changed my dissertation topic again? It's now about phallic symbols in the work of Hugo."

On Friday, Mitchell came to see me in the computer lab before he was done cleaning.

"What would you think about going to a movie or something tonight? You know, so we aren't just fucking every time." His head poked through a narrow opening in the door.

"Sure," I said. I was caught off guard. The thought of fucking was exactly what was getting me through the pile of quizzes I was grading.

"Great. I'll text you in an hour or so." He smiled at me and gave me a wink I had never seen before.

We went to see the late show of the newest *Fast & Furious* movie. It was my choice. I find action movies relaxing. Mitchell thought it was dumb, but I think he just felt bad about Palm

Springs, so I didn't take offense. We stayed through the credits until the lights came up, and then I looked at him and smiled. He grabbed my hand and squeezed it a little.

"So...," I said.

"So," he said, "Want to go to my place?"

I did not. I like my own bed. I'm particular that way. Besides, I don't like to be the one who leaves in the morning.

"You know," I said, "I have a lot to do in the morning. And my dogs ... It would really be better for me if we went to my house." I tilted my head to the side, ever so slightly, and smiled.

"Why don't we just forget it for tonight?"

"Why?" I was stunned.

"Because I have a lot to do in the morning too. I have to wax and buff the entire building."

"Well, maybe we should reschedule then. We could change the routine. Maybe tomorrow night. How 'bout I cook you dinner at my place?"

"Maybe. I might be really tired. I'll call you."

We got up and walked out to the theater parking lot. Mitchell walked me to my car and gave me a hug good-bye.

"Call me early so I know whether to cook or not," I said, as I stepped into the car.

He waited until I was pulled out of my space before he moved.

On Saturday, I read sudden fictions about Sundays. I'd asked my students to start with the word "Sunday" and see what it evoked. Apparently, nothing bad or interesting had ever happened to any of them. Sundays, to most, meant blueberry pancakes for breakfast and the freedom to spend the whole day shopping or playing video games. A few of them wrote about how stressful it was trying to get their work for Beginning Fiction Writing done in time for Monday. I gave them all B-minuses.

By four o'clock, Mitchell still hadn't called. I decided I wasn't going to cook. If he wanted a home-cooked meal, he would have to be more considerate. If he ended up coming over, I would order Thai and make him eat it out of the container.

At six o'clock, I went to the grocery store to buy the ingredients for eggplant parmesan. From the canned food aisle, I called his phone and let it ring thirteen times; his voicemail wasn't set up.

I spent $62 on food and a nice bottle of red and was home by six forty-five. My phone informed me I'd missed a call from Mitchell on the drive home. I stood holding my bag of groceries and listened.

"Sorry I'm calling so late. The floors were really a mess today; they had a department meeting in Philosophy, and there were Rice Krispies treats stuck all over the place. I guessed you'd assume I couldn't make it if I didn't call. I think we need to talk, though. Call me."

I set down my groceries and unpacked the perishables. It was clear that Mitchell was going to break up with me. I took out the eggplant and began to slice it in even, quarter inch-thick slices. I could make the parmesan that night and eat it for the rest of the week. It would be economical.

At eight-thirty, when I was done eating and nearly through the bottle of Pinot, Mitchell called.

"You didn't call me back," he said.

"I was eating dinner."

"What did you have?"

"Nothing," I lied, "Takeout Thai."

"I just grabbed a burger on my way home. I'm wiped."

"Why don't you just say it?" I slopped some wine onto the table as I refilled my glass.

"Say what?"

"Come on," I said.

He took a deep, slow breath. "I don't think we should

see each other anymore. You obviously don't want this to go anywhere. And I just think it would be best if we ended it now, before it gets complicated."

"Uh huh," I said, tasting the sour aftertaste of wine as I exhaled.

"You know, Genevieve, I feel like I really tried with you, but all you seem to be able to manage is fucking and sarcasm."

"Well, then," I said, as if it were a sentence.

"Not that you aren't good at both." I could hear him breathing on the other end of the line.

"I'll see you around then," I said. "We can still be friends. It's not me, it's you. There, I did it for you." I hung up the phone and finished my glass.

On Sunday, I slept until eleven. Then I got up and tried to write a short story about a woman who goes to Palm Springs to meet her boyfriend's parents. I had trouble figuring out her motivation, so I gave up and decided to clean my house. I washed my sheets and cleaned under the toilet seat and got down on my hands and knees to wipe the baseboards. Then I threw away the package of condoms in my nightstand drawer.

On Monday, I returned the Sunday exercises to my class and told them all they had no imagination.

"If nothing interesting has happened to you in your whole life, make something up. Don't write about how nice your family is. Nobody gives a shit," I said, pacing around the room, slapping their stories down on the desks as I passed.

"Blueberry pancakes and cartoons weren't exactly what I meant when I asked you to write about Sundays. Sunday is the day you go back to your mom's after spending the weekend with your dad and his new girlfriend. Sunday is a day of reckoning," I said. "It's simultaneously the end and the beginning. It's for rest and evaluation. It's the day you wake up hungover and full of regret. From now on," I said, "I will accept no happy endings.

I returned to the front of the classroom and looked at them. They avoided my eyes, looked down at their cuticles or at the fraying edges of their notebooks. The world was disappointing because I expected it to be so.

"You're dismissed," I said finally, realizing none of it, nothing really, was their fault.

THE PHLEBOTOMIST'S BOYFRIEND

THIS IS A STORY about my brother, Wade. I'm telling it because he's dead. This is not the story of how he died—that was simple; his truck caught an embankment, flipped, and sent Wade hurtling headfirst into one of those metal dividers. This is the story of what happened before.

I should say that at the time, I wasn't paying that much attention to what was going on. It's only afterward, after Wade is dead, that I try to go back and remember it all. At the time I was starting eleventh grade and sneaking out my bedroom window at night to run across the well-tended lawns of our neighbors and meet Anthony Lorie at the corner of Maple and Ohio, which is just a rounded and sloped piece of sidewalk halfway between our houses. We would go to Round Table, and afterwards, we would go to the dugout at St Joseph's School for Boys and have sex, an act I found painful and disappointing. I was skinny and slope-shouldered, and boys hadn't paid much attention to me before Anthony.

There are a lot of places I could start, but I think I'll just begin with when he met Bonnie, because that's the important part.

Wade liked her immediately. He was bored as hell working at the 7-Eleven, and when he got tired of reading magazines and stealing lottery tickets, he would just sit around waiting for someone interesting to come in. A cop who might talk about his arrests or an old friend from school.

When Bonnie first came in, Wade noticed her right away. I should mention here that she was beautiful. Her mom was from El Salvador, and her dad was white, and she has this outrageous long black hair that hung down her back and framed this heart-shaped brown face of hers. Eyes twinkling. The whole thing. Anyone would say the same. She was older than he was, but not by much. I think she was twenty at the time.

She buys a Coke and some Red Vines and right away starts flirting with him. Nothing sleazy, just talking about the weather, about how hot it is. Picking up her long black hair and waving at the back of her neck. She's wearing a lab coat, and that's when Wade finds out she's a phlebotomist, that she draws blood for a living. Wade makes a face and asks her how she can stand the needles.

"Never bothered me," she answers. And Wade thinks that's so cool. How Bonnie isn't prissy and squeaky about blood. He's interested right away, and when she leaves with her bag of stuff, he calls after her, telling her to come visit more often. Then he smiles, showing a row of the most perfectly white teeth you've ever seen, and she smiles back and waves with her long fingers. He watches her cross the parking lot and go back into the medical building.

The next day, she comes back, and she spends her whole lunch break leaning on the counter eating the free nachos Wade gives her and flirting with my brother. She tells him about visiting her grandma in El Salvador—how she drank only warm orange soda the whole time. She tells him about her parents, who she still lives with, and about the time she went to Lake Tahoe with a big group of friends and got to gamble even though she was only seventeen at the time. She asks about his arm right away. Just like that. Almost no one does. Kids sometimes, or friends, but hardly anyone else.

Wade's left hand never happened. His arm ends in a smooth stump somewhere between his elbow and the place where his wrist would be. There's a tiny piece of rounded flesh attached to the end of it that I think was supposed to be a thumb but never quite made it.

"Born this way," he says, holding it up so she can see. "Maybe mom ate too many Red Vines when I was inside." He laughs.

Then Bonnie reaches out and touches his arm. Nobody ever does that. Our mom doesn't even like to touch it. But Bonnie just reaches out and runs her beautiful brown hands over the smooth end of it, touching the little start of a thumb. This is the second time they've met.

"Cool," she says. She asks him to bend it so she can see the inside of his elbow. She taps his arm, looking for veins. "I could even draw from this guy." My brother is in love and asks for her phone number, which she gives him.

By the time she comes over and meets our mom and me, Wade calls her his girlfriend. It's been about three weeks, and all we know is that she has this long-ass hair and she's so beautiful, and he loves her so much and blah, blah, blah. She comes over for dinner, and I make this macaroni and hamburger casserole that's really good, and Bonnie helps my mom wash the dishes and says we have a nice kitchen. After, Bonnie and Wade go to get snacks for a movie. After they come back, I watch *Avatar* with them on the couch. They hold hands, look at each other. All lovey-dovey. To tell the truth, I've never seen Wade like this before. He had lots of girlfriends in high school, but they didn't really come over to our house and hang out. They were high school girls, giggly and heavily made-up, and after a while, Wade would get sick of them and break it off. I couldn't really tell if he was going to get sick of Bonnie. Usually I could tell, but not with her.

After the movie, they leave. Me and my mom are in the bathroom brushing our teeth, and she says, "I liked her. What'd you think?"

"She was nice," I say, because she was.

When summer ends, Wade tells my mom he's going to get an apartment with Bonnie. We're having a cookout in our backyard. Just me and my mom and Wade and Bonnie. I'm grilling hot dogs and Bonnie brought this potato salad that she says everyone eats in El Salvador. My mom lets me drink one beer, but she lets Wade have as many as he wants even though he's still only eighteen.

"So," Wade says, his hand on our mom's shoulder, "Bonnie and me are going to look for an apartment somewhere around the new hospital. She thinks she can get a job in the lab." The new hospital is only about ten miles away, but Wade says it like he's moving to New York.

My mom is setting the picnic table with these crappy plastic plates we have for cookouts, and she doesn't turn around or anything. She just keeps setting the table and says, "That sounds good. Where you going to get the money?"

My brother makes $11.13 an hour. I know because I asked. He tells my mom he's been saving, and that Bonnie has been saving too and that in about another month, they will have enough for a deposit plus first and last.

"That sounds good then," my mom says again, and that's the end of the conversation. We sit and eat, and Bonnie asks me about eleventh grade, which is not a very interesting topic of conversation, in my opinion.

One time, before our dad moved away and married another woman and had another set of kids, we went on a family vacation to Los Angeles. I was ten. On the way down, we ate every meal at a different Carl's Jr., breakfast, lunch, and dinner. The drive was long and hot, and I spent the time trying to count the huge, cat-shaped electrical towers. I stopped at a little less than two hundred because Wade tackled me in the back seat and held his hand over my mouth until I promised to cut it out.

When we went to Knott's Berry Farm, the attendant

wouldn't let Wade go on the water ride because of his hand (which was a stupid reason, and our mother told him so). I insisted on riding it three times. The lines were long, and it was a million degrees out.

When we left the park, my clothes were drenched, and my sneakers made little squishing noises when I walked. I knew Wade was hot and irritated, but I didn't care. Being able to do something he couldn't was one of the best feelings of my life.

Later, when we were at a restaurant having dinner, my father told us that he and my mom were getting a divorce. The whole thing was awful—the news, the sticky plastic booths, the canned Cyndi Lauper song—but what I felt especially bad about was leaving Wade while I went on the water ride over and over. That night, in our room at the motel, I couldn't stop crying.

Wade watched basketball on TV and just kept saying, "I knew it. I totally knew it."

The next day, we drove back home without our father. Turned out he was moving to Los Angeles, and the whole trip had been a way of giving him a ride.

In October, instead of moving to a new apartment, my brother spends his whole savings on a ring for Bonnie. A diamond ring—14 karat gold. He takes her out to dinner and then drives her out to the edge of the Bay and proposes to her. Down on one knee, ring box open, the whole thing. Bonnie, though, says no. She is, in fact, mad at him. She says, "What the hell?" which is not at all the answer my brother expects.

"Holy Christ, Wade," she says. "Take that fucking thing back and get your money."

My brother must have been pretty humiliated, down on his knee like that. But the worst part is, he can't take the ring back. It never occurred to him that Bonnie would say no. The ring was on sale for $999 when he bought it, and the guy was clear: no returns,

He can't tell Bonnie. He loves her too much and he's really just fucking embarrassed as hell.

He tells her he'll take it back, and then she tells him that it's not because she doesn't love him, just that she isn't ready yet. She wants them both to have good jobs and their own apartment and also, when they do get married, she wants rose gold, not yellow gold.

By Halloween, all me and my mom know is that Wade has still not moved out. He never tells us about the proposal or the ring or any of it. We don't see Bonnie for about two weeks, which is a really long time because usually she comes over almost every day. Then, one day, Wade gets a new truck. Well, a new used truck, but it's nice. It's a Ford and it's red and it still looks good even though it's about ten years old.

Once he gets the truck, everything changes. He starts acting happy again, like his regular self. He loves his truck and will even drive me and my friends' places just so he can be in it, going somewhere. He's still working at 7-Eleven, only now he's the day manager which means he makes $14.59 an hour and knows the combination to the safe.

Wade robs the 7-Eleven because Bonnie thinks he got his money back for the ring when really what he got was his truck. He traded the ring to this guy Steve for the truck so Steve could propose to *his* girlfriend. Wade is stalling on moving in with Bonnie, and Bonnie is getting pissed about the whole thing. It's already November, and they're both still living with their parents. My brother is about to have his nineteenth birthday.

It isn't that hard to do. He just opens the safe and takes some cash. Not all of it, but enough for first and last month's rent. Something like a thousand dollars, enough to make up for the ring, which is now a truck.

But it's the stupidest robbery of all time because after they figure out the night manager didn't do it, Wade is the first and only suspect. The cops arrest him at work while the Iranian guy who owns the place yells at him in the parking lot. Bonnie misses the whole thing because she's in the lab drawing blood from this cancer patient who hardly has any veins left at all.

When Wade calls from the police station, I answer the phone. All he says is to call mom and tell her he's in jail, which is what I do. Then I call Anthony Lorie, who I've never asked a favor of, and ask him to drive me to the jail.

Our father visited us once after he moved to LA. It was maybe a year since our trip to Knott's Berry Farm. Our mother drove us to meet him at the Sizzler in Vallejo. She dropped us off in the parking lot and said to call her when we were ready to come home.

Our father was waiting for us in the lobby. He looked tan and bright-eyed, and he wore a Hawaiian shirt with big hummingbirds all over it. When he hugged us, we tried not to notice the stuffed ballerina teddy bear and the Dodgers cap that were so obviously gifts for us. We felt shy and quiet, and when it was time to order, I picked the cheapest thing on the menu.

"Don't be silly," our father said, grinning at the girl behind the counter as if they were in on a joke. "You always want the fried shrimp. Why don't you get the all-you-can-eat."

I shrugged and said, "Okay" in this tiny voice that didn't at all sound like me. Wade got a steak well done, just like our dad ordered.

When we sat down, he took some pictures out of his wallet. A tiny baby girl with a pink bow attached somehow to her almost non-existent hair. "This is your sister, Emily," he said, smiling down at the photo in his tanned hands.

At first, I thought he was kidding, or confused. We had no sister Emily. It didn't make a bit of sense. I looked at Wade. He was peering down at the photo with interest.

"She's cute," he said, looking up at our dad.

"She is cute, but she's a little hellion. Don't let those baby-blues fool you."

I looked at our father, as handsome as a movie star, and it hit me that this little baby was his new daughter. It felt as if someone were holding me underwater, and I excused myself to go to the bathroom, where I leaned on the counter and stared myself down in the mirror to keep from crying.

When I got back to the table, Wade was wearing his new baseball cap and slathering butter on his baked potato. I looked at the mound of glistening fried shrimp and knew I couldn't eat a single one.

"We should go now," I said.

Our father looked at me and smiled that same jokey smile. "Go? Our food just got here, Sweetie Pie." He cut off a hunk of steak and popped it in his mouth.

"Wade," I said. "I'm calling Mom. I don't feel good." My voice was shrill now, on the edge of panic.

Wade looked at me with a blank face. Neither of us had phones, but there was one in the foyer where I called our mother and told her we were ready to be picked up. I waited on the bench outside the front door where an old lady sat and smoked until I saw our mother's orange Toyota, then I ran into the parking lot and got in the front seat. Our mother went in to get Wade. Our father did not come out to say goodbye.

On our way home, our mother asked how it went. Her voice was bright and light.

"Fine," I said.

"He's an asshole," Wade said, throwing his Dodgers cap out the window and onto the freeway, where it skipped off into the distance.

Bonnie is furious. When she meets us down at the jail, her face is actually red with fury. Her hair is ropy and knotted as if she drove with her head out the window.

"Goddamn you, Wade," she says. No sympathy at all.

He tries to tell her that he did it for her, but even he can tell before he starts that she doesn't care.

"You're gonna get locked up," she says to him before she leaves to go back to work.

The trial is dismal. The court has no mellow glow of polished wood. No low lighting or comfortable chairs. No dignity at all, really. Some lady in a tight red suit that gapes at the chest has her desk pushed right up against the judge's bench, and it's piled high with papers and photos of her kids in ugly frames. Right away, I know Wade is going to jail. The room is all bureaucratic sloppiness, no philosophical musing on the nature of justice. It's a room without sympathy or patience.

For some reason, my brother has elected to shave his head before the trial. He looks like a thug, and as soon as he's sitting up there in that cheap wood box, I can easily see him as the jury sees him: a loser, a danger to himself and society. Even I lose a little respect for him as he sits there mumbling his responses to the barked questions of the prosecutor.

The trial takes one day, and the jury deliberates for about two hours. They're a collection of people who seem to have nothing better to do, people with dull, mean eyes. They pronounce Wade guilty with little fanfare, and the judge says a few words about learning his lesson and sentences him to a year of probation and one month of house arrest, which means he has to wear this ankle tracking device that will alert the police if he leaves our house. My mom has to agree to the set-up, which she does. Bonnie doesn't even show up.

This is how my brother spends his captivity: he sits in the backyard and calls Bonnie about every thirty minutes. She must've told the people at work not to let him talk to her, because after he gets through the first time and she hangs up on him, he never gets through again. He talks to her mother, who tells him she's sorry, but Bonnie says not to call anymore, and he talks to her father who says, "Son, this is not the right thing to do. You will see that someday," and then, after a week of calls, "Damn it, Wade. We're calling the police," which they do.

Wade's probation officer tells him that if he continues to harass Bonnie, he'll request that Wade spend the remainder of his sentence in an actual jail.

My brother loses weight, which I think is strange because whenever I come home from school, he's eating chips and frozen burritos and other crap. His eyes seem to pop out and there's a little rash of acne under each cheekbone. He doesn't look good, but I don't tell him that. He's feeling bad enough as it is.

Every night, if I don't have too much homework, I watch a movie with him. Sometimes, our mom will come in and sit with us on the couch, her feet tucked under her butt, but mostly she stays in her room after dinner, reading or watching something on her iPad. Even with Wade there all the time now, our house seems quiet.

On the day the house arrest ends, Wade drives his truck over to the lab where Bonnie works. He doesn't go in or try to call first; he just drives over at around four and waits in his truck for her to get off.

When she comes out of the peach-colored building, emerging from behind the Medical Offices sign, he realizes he doesn't know what to say. She's alone, and she walks quickly across the parking lot to her old Honda and drives away. Wade just sits there, watching her. She doesn't even notice him.

He isn't drunk when he crashes his car. It's just another accident, like one that happens every day, like the ones they report on the radio. Wade is the guy lying on the side of the road, delaying traffic.

When the hospital calls, my mom and I are in the kitchen washing lettuce. When she hangs up, she leaves the sink full of water, the leaves floating in there like lily pads, and grabs my arm. I know it's something terrible, but it isn't until she's pulled out of the garage and wound her way over to the freeway on-ramp that she says, "Your brother's in the hospital."

A bright light pops somewhere in the back of my head. I start to say, "Oh God" over and over until my mother shushes me.

Wade's in the ER, already practically dead. They need my mother there so that they can pull the plug and use his organs on other people. His head is wrapped in gauze and his eyes are swollen shut. There's a tube taped to his mouth and machines breathe and beep and purr beside him. The black shapes on the floor are his blood, already dried and dull. My mother pulls a chair over to his bed and presses his hand to her forehead. She isn't crying, just sitting there with her eyes closed and Wade's hand pressed to her head like a washcloth.

I'm standing against the door looking at him with something that feels like disgust. I think about how I will act when he gets home. I'll be nicer, more talkative. I leave the room to call Bonnie. She'll be sorry now, I think.

It takes forever for her to come to the phone, and when she does, she says, "What?" like I've interrupted something important. The linoleum gleams beneath my feet, and I watch my silhouette in it as I speak.

"I just thought you would want to know that Wade's in the hospital."

She sighs.

"He's going to the ICU."

I can hear her swallow and then she asks, in the laziest voice you can imagine, what happened.

"He crashed his truck on the freeway. He totaled it. I think he's going to die." My voice swings into a whine, and I start to cry. When I start, I can't stop. Bonnie is listening to me on the other end, and I just stand there crying into the phone, unable to form words.

"Should I come?" she says.

"No," I choke back. "It's your fault." Then I hang up the phone. I hate her so much it burns, but I hate myself more for not knowing to hate her sooner.

When I go back into Wade's room, my mother is standing away from the bed with her arms folded. A doctor and two nurses are checking the machines, injecting something into one of his IVs.

"Say goodbye to your brother," she says, as if he's leaving on vacation, going away to camp. I stare at her from the doorway. "Say goodbye to Wade, Cassie."

I'm very tired, and when I go to my brother, it is as if I'm in one of those nightmares in which I can't move my feet. I'm afraid I'll fall, and I brace myself against the side of his bed. I can't look at his swollen face, the eyelashes crusted with bits of dried blood or the stretched, yellow sheen of his cheeks. I take his arm, cradling the smooth stump of a hand in my own. It's warm and alive, and I stroke the place where a hand should be, touching the little thumb, running my hand up to the smooth skin on the inside of his elbow.

My mother nods and then comes and takes Wade's good hand. The doctor detaches the respirator from Wade's mouth, leaving the end of the blue tube sticking up like a snorkel from his lips. He dies gently, and we don't know he's gone until the doctor puts his hand on my mother's shoulder and says, "You have done a brave and generous thing."

My mother lays Wade's hand across his chest, and I do the same with his other arm. On our way out, she signs some papers. His heart, his liver, his kidneys, they can take what they want.

I stand at the nurse's station, watching them in my haze. "My brother," I want to tell them, "My brother just died." Then a thought comes, something to make them notice him, to make them care that he's gone. "His girlfriend is a nurse," I say. My mother looks at me and squints. She's crying now, and I expect her to correct me. Instead, she grabs my hand and says my name, "Cassandra," like a whisper.

A REASON FOR EVERYTHING

We spent the first four days of our trip visiting churches and museums and buying badly made versions of nice things—a fake Gucci purse, a glass fountain pen for five euros, various carnival masks with little flourishes of metallic paint. Owen's mother, Lo, who wore pale pink sweatsuits that were only distinguishable from one another by the various appliqués on the front, had attached herself to the idea of buying what she referred to as classy Italian clothes. In boutique after boutique, she would ask, her speech distorted by the weird Italian accent she'd picked up during her stay, if the clothes came "mas grande." She was a large woman whose breasts formed a long slow slope to her waist. The impossibly stylish girls who worked at the boutiques would smile apologetically and say no, and we would leave, but not without hearing Lo wonder aloud why they weren't showing her size in Italy that year.

My own mother, who had been to Venice as a college student thirty-five years before, spent our meandering journeys through the city exclaiming that, yes, Venice certainly had changed, or swearing, just swearing, that was the same fountain where flocks of handsome Italian boys had asked to buy her gelato in 1969. "I wonder what he's doing now," she would ask dreamily after one of her Italian admirer stories and then she would add, sighing, "He's probably married; they all are." She led us—poor, huffing Lo and all—on treks through winding alleys in search of cafés where she once spent afternoons drinking espresso and reading. Owen and I made jokes at night about the tours of questionably significant places.

On the fifth morning of the stay, we met in the hotel restaurant for our usual breakfast of crusty rolls and jam. Lo showed up first, and when we asked where Greta was, she shrugged and said primly, "It's none of my business."

My mom and mother-in-law shared a room next to ours and usually came down together. "Well, is she coming for breakfast?" I asked. Lo shrugged again. She could be like that, huffy and prissy as a nun.

Later, as we sat sipping our cappuccinos and sharing sections of the *Herald Tribune*, my mother appeared.

"Hello," she said, standing over our table and bending slightly as if she were bowing.

"Good morning, Greta," Owen said, pulling out a chair for her. "Sleep late?" My stockinged feet were resting on his lap, and I reluctantly removed them so my mother could sit down.

She giggled. "I can't stay, actually," she said. "I have plans. I've met someone. A man."

Owen raised his eyebrows.

"All *I* know is that she wasn't in our room this morning," Lo said. It came out in a rush, as if she'd been dying to tell us, pressing her lips together to keep the words from tumbling out.

My mother smiled again. "It's true," she said, shrugging.

"Who is he?" I sounded suspicious even to my own ears.

"His name's Mauro. He's from Milan." My mother looked around the restaurant for spies, leaned closer, and whispered, "He's younger."

"I don't get it. Where'd you meet him?"

"At the bar. Last night. After you all went to sleep."

"*I* wasn't asleep," Lo said.

"He's taking me to Lido today. His brother has a boat there. We're going boating." She tried to say this as if boating off the coast of Italy with an Italian admirer wasn't the biggest thrill of her life.

"That sounds great," Owen said. "Have a great time. And remember, use a condom."

"Owen!" we all said at once. And then my mother winked at him, turned, and went out the door into the bright Venetian day.

After she left, we sat in silence for a moment until Owen said, "It kind of makes visiting the old prison sound awful, doesn't it?"

Despite the grimness our itinerary for the day had taken on, we stuck to it. We took a ferry to the prison and toured it dutifully. It was a gloomy, dripping place that smelled of sewer gasses, and as we made our way through its curving tunnels, I knew we all wished ourselves afloat on the sparkling sea, a glass of cold pinot grigio in our hands. My mother's date was quietly, without mention, ruining our day.

Each night we were the first diners to appear in whatever restaurant we went to. Sometimes, by the time we were paying the check, a particularly uncool Italian family with children in tow would just be sitting down, but mostly, we were finished with our tartuffes and waddling back to the hotel before even the smallest Italian toddler began to whine for his dinner. I hoped the waiters attributed it to jet lag, and I made a big production of yawning, sometimes even mysteriously mimicking an airplane with my arms by way of apology as we showed up at the first sign of dusk.

"We're *Americans*," my mother would say to me, implying, I supposed, that we could do anything we wanted, that the Italians would love us even as we moved like big slow children through their city buying the wrongs things, eating at the wrong time, and clumsily ordering cappuccinos after ten a.m.

Now, even though we'd spent two hours lunching on roast rabbit and sautéed spinach, we were ready for dinner by six-thirty. The problem we faced wasn't our unfashionably early appetites, but the fact that my mother had not yet returned from her date. It had been almost ten hours since we let her skip off with the anonymous Mauro from Milan; surely she must be sunburned and tired and ready to return to us by now.

We were of two minds. I thought we should wait until eight. Lo and Owen thought we should go on without her. If she came back while we were at dinner, she could eat at the hotel. Besides, she was probably dining with Mauro. "I'd be surprised if we saw her before tomorrow morning," Lo said, picking a long hair off the front of her blouse. Throughout the beginning of the trip, it occurred to me in bright, humiliating flashes, that my mother and Lo didn't really like each other much. I started to suspect they only tolerated one another because Owen and I were married, and they were both single.

When we returned to the hotel, the man at the front desk waved me over with his white-gloved hand and handed me a piece of the hotel's stationery on which he had transcribed a message from my mother. It said, "Meet you tomorrow at breakfast." I thanked him and smiled and followed Lo and Owen to the squeaky old wrought iron elevator.

We often found ourselves returned too early. It was barely nine and we were back in our rooms while in the piazza below us children squealed and glasses clinked. Owen was making his way through *Ulysses*, and he took our early nights as an opportunity to get a lot of reading done.

"Let's go out," I said.

He was changing into his pajamas, and he stopped unbuttoning his shirt, shrugged and said, "Okay." He was agreeable in the same way he was handsome: without a hint of calculation.

We wandered through the Piazza San Marco, through the throngs of Japanese tourists and other American couples, with the vague notion of finding a jazz club. In our imaginations there existed a small downstairs bar full of smoke and sweaty musicians where we could drink Italian beer and hang out with the locals. We held hands and stopped to kiss, and there were quick, fleeting moments when the feeling of being away, of really being somewhere else, would wash over me, filling me, for the first time in a long while, with an intoxicating sense of anticipation.

At one point we went into a place called Club Be Bop. Inside, groups of preteens giggled and sipped cokes and moved in great undulations, like flocks of starlings. The only person over twenty was the guy behind the bar who talked on his cell as he served sodas.

By eleven, we were exhausted. We had, after all, been on our feet all day. We stopped at a sidewalk café where we were given menus in English, something that always made me mad despite the fact that I didn't know Italian. From the tiny marble-topped table we could sip our warm Moretti and watch other tourists meander along the cobblestone walkways. The shop across from us was open and doing a brisk trade in the colorful candy-shaped glass I had resisted buying for the last five days.

"I don't think it's our fault," Owen said, as I took my first, bright sip of beer.

"What's not?"

"Oh, you know, just everything. I don't think it's our fault that all we can find are tourist places, places my mother would like. I think maybe Venice is just sort of an inauthentic place now."

"But people live here. *They* don't eat overcooked pasta and pay twelve euro for a beer." I took another long drink. "I don't know, I know that somewhere in this city someone is having a better trip than us."

"Your mother, for one."

I laughed. "Don't remind me."

"You should be glad for her. She's been trying to meet a man for twenty years. This'll make her happy." Owen swirled his beer in its glass.

"Quit being so kind, Owen; it makes me feel like shit. How would you react if your mother took up with some playboy?" I finished my beer and waved at the bored-looking waiter to bring us two more.

"Do you really think that's possible?" Owen said, sitting up in his chair, "Maybe Mauro has a friend!"

"That actually would be kind of great."

"It would, in actual fact, be a miracle."

The next morning my mother was late for breakfast, again. Lo informed us, as she huffed into the restaurant, her powder-pink sweatsuit shushing as she walked, that Greta hadn't returned until that morning.

"She's showering," she said, and then added, under her breath, "which is probably a good thing."

When my mother did appear, she had composed her face into a façade of nonchalance, even going so far as to not notice as we sat gawking at her from our table. She sat, spread her napkin on her lap, and raised her eyebrows as if to say "what?"

"Well," Owen said, leaning toward her like a nosey girlfriend.

"Well, what?" Her face opened and beamed. "We had a very nice time," she said, lowering her face with a gaudy display of false modesty. This was a woman who lived as a nudist in Florida for three years. She wasn't shy.

"I'm so happy for you, Greta. That's just great," Owen said, patting her hand. Lo and I made murmuring noises of agreement.

The waiter came to take her order, a cappuccino and a sweet roll. We ordered another round and then sat arranging our silver-ware and smoothing our napkins.

"When do we get to meet this Mauro fellow?" Owen said,

sounding ridiculously fatherly and pompous. "Shall we invite him to dinner?"

"Done," my mother said. "I assumed it would be fine. He's offered to take us to a very out of the way place."

Owen and I exchanged glances across the table. His, I believe, meant, "Great, now we'll see the authentic Venice." Mine meant, "Great," as in "Fuck," but I'm pretty sure my husband misread it.

In my heart of hearts, I believed it was good for me to be married to such a reliably nice guy, that being with a man who wrote poetry and whose glass was forever half full of the purest spring water functioned as a sort of counterbalance to my twin predilections towards worry and disgust. But there were also those times when I wanted to wipe that twinkling smile right off his face, when more than anything, I needed him to join me in my dismal little cave. This was one of those times. His unfaltering cheer was getting on my nerves.

After my third cappuccino, I announced my departure from the table. Our sixth day, the two-thirds mark, was a free day. We had nothing planned: no tours, no meals, no museums. I had the nebulous idea of spending the morning alone, wandering the streets with my sketchbook. I was no artist, but I had long wished to return from a trip with one of those lovely, illustrated journals under my arm like a 19th-century voyager. I was hoping to find some beautiful fountains from which I could make tiny watercolor renderings. Owen was going to go to the old library to read and poke around. Our mothers could shop, rest, do whatever they wanted. As I got up to prepare for my day of painting and gentle contemplation, my mother rose and announced that she thought she'd join me.

Once we were outside and making our way into the twisting old alleyways of Venice, she clutched my arm. "I'm so happy we have this time alone. I've been dying to talk to you." I smiled and patted her arm. "Can you believe this thing with Mauro? I'm sixty-one years old! I thought grandchildren were the only thing I had to look forward to—sorry, but it's true—and then we come to Venice, and bam, I fall in love."

I stopped in front of a trinket shop and faced her. I didn't know where to begin. This trip with our mothers, our first since we'd given up on the prospect of parenthood, was in some ways, a booby prize for Lo and Greta. Facing an old age bereft of grandchildren had left them both feeling shaken and cheated. They tried to be supportive, but I couldn't help feeling as if each of my periods was a form of filial treachery. Taking them to Venice was an apology of sorts. What we meant to say was, "Sorry about that whole lack of grandchildren thing, but look, a whole city built on water!"

What I said was, "You fall in *love*? Mom, you've known him for two days. You're *not* in love."

"Ah, ah, ah," she said, wagging her finger at me. "The older you get, the sooner you know."

We turned a corner and sat on the edge of a fountain whose cherubs were black and disintegrating with age. I didn't know what I was thinking with the sketchbook; everything in Venice had been painted and drawn and photographed to death. I could never have captured anything new.

"I just don't know how you can possibly know he's the one after, what, thirty-six hours."

"Oh, phooey. I don't believe in the *Ladies Home Journal* crap. There are a hundred ones, a thousand. Part of getting what you want is deciding you have. And I've decided."

I couldn't pinpoint the moment when my mother turned into this type of irrepressibly positive middle-aged woman—the kind who bought books of daily meditations and drank ginkgo biloba smoothies and made dinner dates with women who visited psychics and went on singles trips to Costa Rica. My memories of her from childhood were of a frazzled, frantic woman, a woman who put her mascara on in the car while she drove me to school and screamed at me when I forgot to pack my own lunch. I didn't know exactly how to respond to her new brand of positive vibes.

"Well then," I said, linking my arm through hers, "I can't wait to meet him."

I was nervous about what to wear to dinner. Italians seemed to know things about clothes that I wouldn't even have thought to wonder about. I was convinced, for example, that Mauro would be able to tell that my stockings were from the drugstore and that my diamond studs weren't actually diamonds at all. My mother had assured us, as Mauro had assured her, that where we were going wasn't a dressy restaurant, that we would be able, as he put it, to go in dungarees. Still, I felt the need to put on a good face, and so we dressed, not too much, but enough so that I wouldn't feel like a stupid American. Even Lo, we discovered when we met in the lobby, had gone to some trouble. Her hair was fluffed into a cotton-candy-like halo around her head and, much to my horror, she had pinned a rhinestone American flag to her bosom. My own mother wore the loose-fitting dress favored by women of a certain age in Northern California. Her idea of dressing up was a shapeless cotton dress and some giant piece of jewelry made by indigenous people.

Mauro was picking us up at eight, and we were all in the lobby fifteen minutes early. My mother and I ordered glasses of sour red wine and leaned against the bar gulping them silently. Owen and Lo sat side by side on one of the uncomfortable benches, their hands folded in their laps.

At eight-fifteen, my mother ordered us two more glasses of wine and a little dish of olives. Owen joined us at the bar, tossing olives into his mouth like peanuts. "You know Italians," my mother said, "They have a very relaxed sense of time." She smiled and twisted her necklace into a knot. Lo stayed on the bench, staring straight ahead in her Midwestern way.

When Mauro showed up at a quarter to nine, Lo was yawning, and my mother was one glass of wine into tipsy.

I'd imagined a cascade of silver hair rising from the sunglassed, angular face of an Italian movie star, all tanned skin and straight teeth. At first, as Mauro approached my mother and kissed her on the cheek, I experienced a moment of intense confusion, thinking that somehow my mother knew someone else in Venice who just happened to be walking through the lobby of our posh hotel. Mauro was portly. That was the word that came to mind. Round and shiny with a thinning ruff of jet-black hair circling his skull. He wore a pink linen shirt that stretched so tightly across his middle little tuffs of black hair escaped through the gaps.

In the swirl of kisses and handshakes that followed, I was reminded of the receiving line at our wedding, of the intense ache of my smile and the inability to focus on any one face. When we were done with the introductions and greetings, the expectant silence of a group of nervous strangers descended.

"Well," my mother offered cheerfully, her eyes darting between our faces, "Shall we go?"

She held Mauro's arm as we walked.

"It must be so wonderful for you to see where your mother spent so much time as a signorina. This is your first time in Venice, no?" he asked, as we trotted down the darkened streets.

"Yes," I said, wanting to explain that although I had not been to Venice, I was no rube. For the first three years of our marriage, Owen and I traveled. Twice a year we took two weeks off and went somewhere: Argentina or Costa Rica or Amsterdam or Sicily. We spent a week in Tunisia; we strolled the avenues of Paris and Cologne and Budapest. We ate iguana stew in Mexico. Then we decided it was time to have children. For the next three years, we stayed home, mating unsuccessfully.

"And how do you find it? Beautiful, no?"

"It's a bit touristy but yes, it's exquisite."

"Ah, yes, many tourists. But you do not blame us for this. We make something beautiful, everybody want to come see it. The curse for Italians is to love beauties too much." He looked at my mother, who fluttered her eyelashes and did her best Audrey Hepburn impression, which wasn't really very good.

"No, no. I don't blame anyone for the tourists. It's just too bad that so much of this city is designed for them. You know, we can't find a good place to eat and all."

"Or maybe you just don't know where to look," he said, winking at me.

I fell back in step with Owen and Lo, who was making little tracksuit whispers with her thighs. I took Owen's hand and adjusted my steps to match his.

"He's not what I was expecting," he whispered to me.

"Me neither. And he certainly doesn't look younger."

"He seems just fine," Owen said, squeezing my hand. "You should relax. You're doing that thing with your mouth."

I puckered my lips and exhaled. "I don't know why this is making me so anxious."

Owen shrugged. "People don't like it when their mothers date. It's not so unusual. Just try to keep it in check."

The restaurant was, as promised, very out of the way. It wasn't, as we had hoped it would be, entirely undiscovered. We were given menus in English, and when I asked for some extra fresh tomatoes to go with the mozzarella, I was given a bottle of ketchup, which I took as an insult. But for the most part, it was pleasant and good and relatively empty of tourists.

"So," Owen asked, as we picked through a plate of charcuterie sliced to transparency, "What do you do in Milan, Mauro?"

"I have three shops. Dog grooming. Washing, cutting, make them smell good. I learned in America."

"Oh, you lived in the States. Whereabouts?" I asked.

"New Jersey. You know Jersey City? Almost New York. I have family there. Two cousins." He rolled up a bit of cheese in a slice of mortadella and stuck it into his mouth.

"I've never been to Jersey City," I said, "but I hear it's nice."

"I don't know, but for me, it was not. Three years, then I come home." He raised his finger like he just had an idea "And now I have a good business, so America was good for me." He smiled, proud of himself. It seemed to me that his English was getting worse.

My mother smiled at him adoringly and then flitted her eyes around the table, grinning at us in turn as if the power of her own enthusiasm would rub off. Her teeth were stained a purply gray from so much red wine, but she looked pretty and flushed.

I watched the dog groomer stealthily. As vigorously as I tried to prevent it, I could not keep myself from imagining my mother and the dog groomer *in flagrante*. It was an image that disgusted me, all hairy limbs and the taut roundness of his belly. I was reminded of the time I heard my parents having sex. I was about twelve, old enough to know for sure what was going on, and the sound of their coupling made me frantic with embarrassment. Afterward though, as I faced them at breakfast, I felt powerful over my parents for the first time in my life, distant and aloof, as if I could walk away from them any time I wanted.

Now I felt fiercely protective. I wanted to take my mother's hand and pull her away from Mauro. Not only was she my mother, but this was *our* trip, not his.

"So," Mauro said, as we dug into our respective pasta courses, "Greta tells me you will not have children. For an Italian, this is very sad. For us, they are life. For Americans, I don't know. Maybe this is common." He shoved a massive forkful of tagliatelle into his mouth and chewed with the speed and regularity of a piston.

Owen and I hesitated for a moment, waiting to see which one of us would respond.

"Ah," my husband said, "It's very sad, indeed. If we could change things, we would, but ..." He shrugged and smiled. What could he say?

My mother leaned forward and said, "Oh, but you can. You can change things. I don't understand why you won't adopt!"

"Mom," I said. "We've talked about this. Now is not the time."

"Ah well," Mauro said cheerfully, "You can still change your minds. You do not have to give up hope yet."

Owen and I nodded and returned our attentions to our plates.

My mother and Mauro walked us back to the hotel and then left us, strolling arm in arm into the Venice night.

"Do you think she's right?" I said to Owen as we stood brushing our teeth. My speech was slurred with foam and my breasts jiggled from the violence of my scrubbing.

"About what?" Owen examined his nostrils, checking for the little hairs that had recently begun to protrude like insect legs from his nose.

"About adopting. I feel like I never have a good reason for why we decided not to."

"Because we decided not to. You don't have to have a reason for everything."

"At first we wanted to, though. Sometimes it seems like we just changed our minds, and I can't figure out why."

Owen exhaled and started to undress. "You thought it was a sign. Remember? You thought if we couldn't conceive, it meant we shouldn't be parents."

"I know. But I think I just got scared. I kept thinking we'd get a horrible child who played with fire and hated us. Did you ever see *The Bad Seed*?"

"You're funny," he said without laughing. "All kids hate their parents at some point. You shouldn't let that scare you. And it's not final. If you want, we can investigate it again when we get home. But for God's sake, don't do this for your mother."

"I'm not doing anything for my mother." I stepped out of my

underwear and tucked them into my suitcase. "It's just that not having children makes me feel like a brat."

On our last night in Venice, Lo wanted to go to a special restaurant. It was a place she'd read about in the in-flight magazine on the way over, and she was especially keen on the strolling concertina players. We got there early, of course, but it didn't much matter. It was full of tourists, all of them as bumbling and foreign as we were.

I asked my mother not to invite Mauro, making up some lie about how Lo really wanted it to be just the four of us on the final night of the trip. She sat at the table sulking like a child while good-looking waiters in red vests brought us plates of bland pasta and oily salad.

Over the whine of the concertina music, Owen proposed a toast. "To our mothers, Greta and Lo," he said, raising his glass, "We couldn't ask for better parents or better company."

"Hear, hear," I said, clinking my glass against Owen's.

"I'm not going back with you," my mother said, raising her glass and tipping it against Lo's.

"To the hotel?"

"No. Home. I'm not going home just yet. Mauro has invited me to Milan, and I've decided to go."

"Oh, dear God, you can't be serious," I said, setting my glass down with more violence than I intended.

"Why on earth can't I be serious, Lena?"

"Keep it down, you two!" Lo hissed. "This is a nice place!"

"Mom," I said, lowering my voice, "you have a life back home. You can't just pick up and leave it."

"Who says I'm picking up and leaving it? I'm staying an extra week in Milan and then we'll see what happens."

The red-vested waiters swirling around us blurred and swam, and I leaned back against my chair trying to formulate my next sentence.

"Lena," Owen said, patting my shoulder blade, trying, I could tell, to keep the peace. God forbid I make a scene.

"I'm fine," I hissed.

Lo, who had been staring into her plate, determinedly cut her pasta into manageable lengths, sighed, and set her mouth. My mother and I were too much for her—too loud, too emotional, just too Californian for her in general.

I blew my nose into one of the cloth napkins and looked up. A circle of men dressed in green vests and blousy white shirts had collected around us. Their waxed mustaches turned up at the ends. The first notes of their song sounded as high and desperate as keening and then as they pushed and pulled their instruments, each one building on the next, their song expanded, swelled, and seemed to glow before us like a fire.

When the song was over, we clapped and smiled, and they glided away to another table of tourists.

"You shouldn't be so sad," my mother said, patting my hand. I knew she was right. What I wanted for myself was her faith in the goodness of things. But I was a heretic, a person who had not yet accepted the universal truth that there was little difference between being happy and deciding that you were.

Lo finished her pasta and arranged her knife and fork on the plate. "You know what I'm looking forward to?" she asked, joining the conversation for the first time. "The all-you-can-eat salad bar back home. I can't get enough of that tuna pasta salad."

My mother raised her glass. "To the all-you-can-eat salad bar, a truly magnificent American invention."

"Hear, hear," we agreed, raising our glasses in unison.

PIECES OF STRING
TOO SHORT TO USE

My daughter is crazy about the theater. Standard suburban stuff—community productions of *Bye Bye Birdie* and *Oklahoma*. Right now, she's playing Maria in *West Side Story*. She tucks her shaggy blond hair into a black wig and shakes her hips in what she imagines is a Puerto Rican style. She's eleven, and on her chest, there are two bumps the size of chocolate chips. When she kisses me now, and it happens less and less, she takes my face in her two hands and kisses both cheeks, making loud smacking sounds. "Dahling," she says, all Zsa Zsa Gabor.

My mother is starting to wet the bed. That's what the lady who runs the home told me. She said, "Miss Cooper, she don't go to the toilet in the night no more. We can't be cleaning up that type of thing here." I told Mrs. Sanchez I'd talk to her, that it was probably a one-time thing. But I know I'm only prolonging the inevitable.

I don't speak to my mother about the bed-wetting because today she's speaking Russian. She beams when I come to visit every day after work, and then I wait to see what will come out of her sloppily painted mouth. Today it's Russian. Dr. Meyer told me that it's not uncommon to go back to the language of childhood. My mother is eighty-three years old and hasn't been to Odessa in seventy years. It's the short-term memory that goes first, he says. Great, I think, when I misplace my keys, can't remember the word for thermometer, pick Lucy up late from rehearsal. Great.

Lucy's explaining string theory to me while we sit in McDonald's. Eating here is her reward for visiting her grandmother today. She takes a soggy French fry and wiggles it around frantically.

"Okay, inside us is atoms, and inside atoms are protons and electrons and this one other thing I can't remember the name of."

"Neutrons," I say, although honestly, I'm not sure. Are there neutrons in humans?

"Yeah, neutrons," she says back without losing her pace. "And inside those are quarks—don't you think that's kind of a cute name? Quark?" She takes a sip of orange soda, and I can't believe I let her drink that stuff. "And inside *that*," she says, pausing for effect and shaking the French fry furiously now, "are little strings of energy. But they're so microscopic we will never be able to see them. Ever. But the scientists know they're there." She eats the French fry, and I have one of those motherly surges of affection that feels like a crush.

"Never say never," I say. "All sorts of things happen."

She shrugs and sips her soda.

Then she says, "I think some people's strings move fast, some's don't. Like, I have a lot of energy so I'm pretty sure I have fast strings."

Earlier that evening, my mother called Lucy "Eugenia," her sister's name. And Lucy took it in stride, holding her grandmother's face in both hands and kissing each velvety cheek. "Spasibo," she said. It's the only Russian word she knows.

My mother speaks broken English today. "Don't eat. Don't eat," she says, and I understand this is not a command, but a description. When she first moved into the Shady Lane Guest Home, she complained about the mashed potatoes being served with an ice cream scooper. She couldn't think of anything tackier than perfectly spherical servings of mashed potatoes. She cried to me on the phone that first night. That was when she still remembered my phone number.

I should save her somehow. I should let her move in with me or at least bring her the food she likes—herring and olives and tiny tea matzos with French feta cheese. Instead, I leave to pick up my daughter from rehearsal. I go early to sit in the dark auditorium and smell the smell of all that drama and dust and cakey stage makeup.

My daughter wears a purple leotard and black tights. She has the stick-like body of a child. She bumps and grinds, kicks up her heals, purrs out a song in a Puerto Rican accent. She doesn't know I'm there, and I watch like a spy, noting her behavior, watching the way the other kids look at her. I haven't felt this way about someone since I was fourteen and thought every crush would slay me.

When she makes a mistake, she stops what she's doing and stamps her foot, waiting for the music to stop with her and begin again at her cue. Her mistakes are invisible to me, and I'm confused each time she pauses.

When she was five, my ex-husband attempted to explain to her what he likes to call our complicated kinship network. Complicated because after we divorced, he married Lucy's kindergarten teacher, who, in a strange and fated twist, is named Rebecca, like me. His attempt made me glad. Let him struggle through it. And I was proud of my five-year-old daughter when she said to her father, "I get it. I get it."

When I was a child, my mother did community theater. She was pretty good and had her picture in the newspaper every so often.

She played old ladies, gypsies, little Italian nonas. Never the leading lady. My mother didn't have a sexy bone in her body.

She saved everything. "In Russia," she said in her accent-less English, "we sometimes ate the walls. For the calcium. You can't possibly understand." And she would fold pieces of aluminum foil into neat squares and put them back in the drawer. She would rinse out her dental floss and hang it over the bathroom doorknob. In front of my friends! In front of my friends, whose own mothers had hairdos and outfits, and husbands who were always in another room.

When rehearsal is over, the other children sit on the floor changing out of their jazz shoes. Lucy strides over to Tom Mancella, the director, and speaks seriously with him. I can't hear her, but I know she's offering him her ideas. Maybe the dancers shouldn't start until the second bar. Maybe it should go left-right-left instead of the other way around. Tom puts paternal hand on top of her head and ruffles her wig askew. Adults rarely take her seriously enough.

On Fridays, Lucy doesn't have rehearsal, and gets home long before me. This week, when I come home, she's made dinner and lit candles. She waits for me, with a dishtowel over her shoulder like a housewife. There is frozen ravioli with Ragu, a side of pork-n-beans, and "diner toast" wheat toast carefully buttered, stacked, and cut into triangles. I kiss her on the top of her staticky blond head and sit. We love this food, but it worries me how difficult it will be for Lucy to someday find a mate who appreciates her cooking.

"How's Grandma?" she asks between breathy gulps of milk.

I stop and look up at her pale face. I forgot to visit my mother. I just let a whole chapter of my day drop away. It usually goes like this: work, Mom, pick up Lucy, have dinner. I stare at my daughter and a little grunt comes from my throat.

"What?" she says. She's unconcerned, just making conversation between forkfuls of beans.

"I didn't see her today. I forgot."

Lucy looks at me like she's just noticed I'm there. "You forgot?"

I nod.

"Whoa," she says, "You're getting as bad as Grandma."

I grimace and start in on my ravioli. I decide it's okay to forget your mother once in your life.

I'm forty-three years old, and if I can take my daughter out for ice cream after dinner on a Friday night, I have a social life. We know the scooper, Carlos. He goes to the high school, and he calls Lucy "ma'am" and me "miss," and we both harbor crushes. Sometimes, out of nowhere, Lucy will ask, "I wonder what Carlos is doing." Her crush might be worse than mine

Lately, Lucy has been asking me to dye my hair. She's of the opinion that the gray in it makes me look older than I am. My mother really was old when I was born, and for as long as I can remember, she's worn her curly, lead-gray hair cropped short. She's tiny and wiry, and in the 60s, she favored bright muumuus and dashikis. She was one of those mothers who everyone claimed to wish they had. Little did they know. She charmed people against my will.

When I was Lucy's age, I cared only for horses. My obsession was as deep and singular as faith, and my mother shared none of it. Their size made her nervous, and she did her best to get out of their way. She was small and Russian and knew nothing of cowboys and rodeos and the spangled shirts I coveted. To my mother, spangled shirts were meaningless. All those sequins would make them useless to polish furniture with when the shirts got old.

On Saturday morning, Lucy and I stop at the market and buy my mother some treats. It's a bright spring day. Lucy picks out a bunch of daffodils, and I get tea matzos, French feta cheese, and cold, hard Red Delicious apples. My mom is proud of her strong teeth. "All original," she says, grimacing to show them.

The Shady Lane Guest Home is built around a courtyard. We pass through it, past the old men sitting silently in the patches of sun. Except when it rains, these men are a constant. I wonder if they see the nothing happening that I see, or if they have become somehow more excited by the subtle shifting of shadows or closing of petals. I wave to them as I do every day, and they wave back. "Hello, my dear," calls Simon. Poor Simon, sharp as a tack.

The last trip I took with my mother was to the coast. We rented a little house on the jagged edge of the Pacific and spent the weekend walking on the beach, looking at the tide pools. My mother, who always knew the names of things—California Buckeye and fiddleneck and nudibranch—poked her fingers into the bright blue anemones and said absently, "Just like that," each time. She has become guileless, lost her intentional charm. Soon, she will have to be moved to a place with more care. Mrs. Sanchez has been preparing me for it for months.

My mother's room is at the south end of the courtyard. It's full of books she can no longer read and photos of people she knows she should recognize, but doesn't. She has no friends left. All those big bohemian personalities, the gnarled fingers crusted in turquoise, the men with their union pins and striped French sailor shirts are dead or living in their own rest homes, the kind of bourgeois blandness they never imagined for themselves.

When we open the door, the room is dim, and my mother is sitting in her chair looking dead. Her head lolls.

Lucy gasps and clutches my arm. "Mom!" she says quickly.

I put my hand on hers, and we stand like that in the doorway for a few seconds. Nothing teaches you how to protect your daughter from your mother's death.

Then I go to her and do what I've seen other people do. I hold her wrist and put two fingers into the crepey skin on the side of her neck. The pulse is there, same as ever. My mother opens her eyes, drowsy and disoriented. I take her hand with its onion-paper skin and press the cool back of it to my cheek. Lucy comes towards us and then throws herself into my mother's lap. "Your strings are working," she says.

"Oh, for Heaven's sake, get off!" my mother says, sounding exactly like herself. "What's the fuss?"

We let go and begin to unload our bounty in her small kitchenette. "We brought goodies," I say, my heart thudding idiotically.

My mother claps her hands together and gets herself out of the armchair. "We should put it on the fancy china." Then she remembers and laughs. "But of course, I don't have any. I was never that type, you know."

My mother loves it when Lucy comes; it rouses her into more of her old self, charismatic and performy. An old boyfriend once said, "It must be hard having a charm vortex for a mom." Indeed. But it was better than the alternative, a mom who can't remember who I am, a mom disinterested in the present.

We sit down to our mini feast at the small oak table that has followed my mother from place to place since before I was even born.

"When we were in Catalina Island, we had a pet goat, you know," she says, turning to Lucy. "We called him Stinky Bum." She waits for Lucy to laugh, forgetting that Lucy has heard the story of Stinky Bum a hundred times by now. "He wasn't at all stinky, though. He was sweet as can be and he liked to sail. He would even swim in the ocean."

Next, she will tell us about the parties, about dressing up as a gypsy to tell the fortunes of the rich and famous. The punch line: "They're a lot older in person!"

We eat like we love to, little plates of delicacies. My mom tells Lucy the story again of the ship that brought her to America. It's a story I've heard so many times it's in my cells. But my mother lights up as if she's been jump-started. And for a moment I think, maybe it isn't as bad as I thought.

THE GOOD PEOPLE OF
LAKE GEORGE

AT THE LAKE, IT's all her father's friends, people from New York who dress too well for Vermont and complain about the food. Bland bread. No bagels. You must import your own wine. They are funny people with book-lined shelves and a collection of music that spans many generations. Their haircuts are relentlessly good. Celeste has always liked them, but ever since her move to San Francisco, they exhaust her. She's spent the three days since her arrival at the lake house draping herself over the furniture and trying to read old *New Yorkers*.

The lake itself shimmers like a piece of aluminum foil someone has crumpled and tried to flatten out again. It's too cold to go swimming. The boat is broken. People sit around on the deck reading *The Atlantic Monthly* and drinking cup after cup of the good coffee, imported from New York via a fair-trade company in Nicaragua, until it's cocktail hour when they switch first to gin and tonics and then to wine, whatever Harry brings up from the basement.

Celeste can spend an amazing amount of time staring. She sits on the deck, or just inside, on the wicker chairs, with a magazine flattened on her lap, watching the subtle shift of light and wind on the surface of the lake. Sometimes, the conversation will turn to her, and she'll have to admit she wasn't paying attention. Her father's friends, each twenty-five years her senior, smile and nod and make little jokes about how someday she will relish time away from her husband; someday all she'll want to do is spend a holiday weekend at the lake while he stays behind working. She smiles back at them because, really, what's she supposed to say?

Celeste sleeps in the shrine room on a fold-out couch that is more comfortable than her bed at home. At night, she lies between the soft cotton sheets and studies the shrine: incense, candles, Buddha, two color photographs of their teacher with his wide, shining, Tibetan face. There are things she cannot identify, little significant trinkets. A short, knobbed piece of black wood above the door. A painting of a fierce black god with many arms. Some chocolate kisses in a dish of uncooked rice. She thinks this must be an offering. She knows just enough to know that she doesn't know very much. But still, her father calls her a Buddhist; he tells her she's a natural Buddhist at heart. And she feels included and proud, as if she really does belong to these people and their witty opinions and good-quality things.

She inventories the shrine because she knows it will be a long time before Harry comes. He's still up talking to her father about jazz and when they're through, he'll have to wait until he's sure everybody in the house is asleep before he creeps across the wide wood planks of his summer home into the shrine room where she sleeps. She doesn't like to fall asleep before he arrives, so she waits up, letting her eyes grow accustomed to the light from the bright Vermont moon and listening to her father claim that Thelonious Monk was not only a genius but something of a Bodhisattva. They've moved on to Scotch now, and she can hear the ice clink as he sips.

Harry is getting loafy. His summer tanned legs are still strong and muscular, but his torso is thickening, and his shoulders are becoming soft. His chest hair is turning white, and it sticks out of his collar as if he's been flocked. Still, he's handsome. Celeste studies him when she believes no one is watching, and she decides he's handsome because he believes he is. This is his house and his wine cellar and his music collection. Pretty little Robin with her perfectly straight blond bob and her flat, flat stomach that long ago produced two athletic sons, is also his. He's charming and magnanimous. If you're at his house, he will give you anything.

Still, despite his generosity, his opulence, people talk about him behind his back. He's arrogant. He's way too opinionated in a group full of too-opinionated people. They don't like his book collection; it's pretentious and there's speculation about how much he actually reads. If he weren't such a wine snob, dinner would be so much more relaxed. Why must he act as if he is teaching everybody all the time?

Her father takes turns defending Harry and criticizing him. They pick at each other like adolescent brothers, not like men in their deepening middle age, men with bad backs and sagging cheeks.

"Lighten up," Celeste can hear Harry say in the living room. And her father responds, "You lighten up. I'm just saying something that you don't want to hear, so you're getting aggressive."

Once, when they were driving home from the lake, Celeste's father told her "Harry is the best friend I've ever had or ever will have. I just wish I liked him better."

There's no clock in the shrine room, but Celeste thinks it must be nearing two by the time she hears Harry's heavy footsteps tiptoeing across the house. She wonders, as she often does, how many other people know what's going on and then immediately shakes her head to rid herself of that thought. He opens the door, and she can see his bulky frame in the dim light of the moon. He's naked except for his boxer shorts, which further emphasize his loaf-like shape. He slips in beside her and slides a heavy hand across her exposed stomach. Celeste thinks they will not have sex. Harry is too drunk, and this affair is seven years old already, and petering out. Their sex life has thinned, and even though she's moved across the country and they hardly see one another, there's little urgency between them anymore.

"Your father," he says to her, and she can smell red wine. A Burgundy from the eighties was what they were drinking when she went to bed.

"Shh," she says, turning toward him and cupping his jaw.

"Sorry. But God, I thought he'd never shut up. I missed you terribly this past month."

Celeste smiles and leans in to kiss his cheek. Harry turns and presses his lips to hers, breathing heavily through his nose. She's amused by his sudden passion; she knows he's making the effort for her benefit. It's his constant fear that he's not satisfying her.

"I missed you, too," she says, "California is so far away."

"Oh shit. I hate to be reminded. *California* of all places. I can never picture you there. Aren't you a bit smart for them?"

"Not smarter, but definitely meaner."

Harry laughs and moves his head away from hers to get a better look at her in the dim, gray light. "And who is this Ian fellow, anyway? How is it that he could steal you away from me?"

Celeste wished many times in the last few days that Ian had been able to come with her to the lake. Instead, he's in San Francisco, their new home, living the resident's life of no sleep, bad food, case after case of things Celeste finds disgusting: infections and boils—raw, moist things not meant to be exposed.

It's so hard to explain her father's friends to him out of context. She tried over the phone the night before to tell him about the spontaneous dance party they'd had in the living room. How they kicked off their shoes and danced raucously to Aretha Franklin and later, after they switched from wine to brandy, how they sang along with old protest songs, belting out "try to love one another right now" into the still Vermont night. She thinks of Ian sitting in their small apartment in that beautiful city. In her mind's eye, he was smiling, but she's sure he doesn't quite get it, that there is some essential quality about these people he doesn't understand.

"He's my husband, and you've met him. You might remember our wedding, or then again, you probably don't." Harry had passed out well before the dancing began.

Harry turns toward the shrine, taking it in for a few moments and then changing the subject. "If that were a crucifix instead of a Buddha, we wouldn't be able to do what I hope we're going to do in here." He drops his head back against the pillow and sighs.

Unlike most of the people in what her father refers to as "the community," Harry is not Jewish. His family is Irish, what he likes to call "the Jews of Catholicism." Eight children, complete with priest, dead father and drinking problems. Celeste met his mother once at his and Robin's apartment in New York. She was a brisk, sour woman dressed all in black, clutching a rosary. A distinctly un-American kind of lady, whose whole life was a bitter lament for a country she hadn't seen in over fifty years. Robin referred to her as "the weeping Mick," a nickname that caused Harry to frown at his pretty wife whenever she used it.

"If that were a crucifix, we wouldn't be here in the first place. I don't know a single practicing Catholic. They scare me."

"That's your mistake," he says, sliding his hand over her breast and leaning down to kiss her again. "Catholics are safe. It's the Buddhists you have to watch out for."

On Saturday, Celeste, her father, Robin, and Mariah, an old friend from the community who talks too much and spends most of the day in pajamas, decide to go for a hike in the White Mountains. Harry, who does not have the patience for group outings, decides at the last minute to stay home. Nobody objects. He would be intolerable anyway.

The four of them drive through the crazy green hills of Vermont and New Hampshire ensconced in the plush leather seats of whatever luxury car Robin is driving that summer. The stereo plays Bach softly and they gossip.

"I so prefer the women," her father says again. "Women are such great conversationalists." He's driving, glancing back frequently at Robin and Mariah as they tell moderately vicious stories about their mutual friends. Celeste, who remembers some of their friends from her childhood and has never met others, drifts in and out of the conversation, preferring to watch the passing thickets of green and consider her situation and how she's going to end her affair with Harry.

"I don't think Dina would mind if they were just fucking. That's their agreement from what I understand. But Karen has become like a wife to him. It's too much, really." The conversation has turned to Karen, Celeste's father's most recent ex-wife. Celeste listens to them and watches her father. His eyes flit back and forth between the road and the rearview mirror in which he can see Robin and Mariah.

He says, "It'll be Karen who gets hurt. I certainly can't see Robert leaving Dina. He won't leave her. We never do." He smiles because this is not true. He left his third wife for Karen. She has a pattern of breaking up marriages.

"I saw them at the Bernstein's Midsummer's Day party. They were completely out in the open. She was like his girlfriend. I think that's just tacky," Mariah says.

"Love is a powerful thing," her father says. "It is what it is."

"I mean," Robin says, as if she's continuing a sentence, "This is just another thing. It might be full of confusion, but it's just another thing." She sits forward and diamonds gleam in her ears.

Celeste folds her arms and concentrates on the blurring green of the roadside. Soon, they will get out of the car, and she can walk ahead, using her youth as an excuse to leave them behind.

"Celeste, I can tell you don't approve," Robin says. She's known Celeste since she was six.

Her father turns toward her. "Approve of what? Are we getting vicious?" He looks at the back seat. "She and Karen have remained friends."

Celeste feels the familiar heat in her cheeks as her throat constricts. "What do you mean 'it is what it is?' Jesus, I'm not trying to be moralistic, but what about being nice? Aren't Buddhists supposed to be nice?"

"You're right," Mariah says. "We should be nicer. God! I'm such a gossip."

"I don't mean *that*," Celeste says, "I mean, shouldn't we disapprove more of things like affairs? Shouldn't we say that they're a bad thing? That people are being hurt?"

Robin exhales through her nose and throws up her hands, "Affairs happen all the time. They are as much a part of life as marriage. *We* just talk about them. Our community isn't afraid to look at things for what they are."

"Life is complicated—painful and complicated—but I can't do conventional morality." Her father leans forward as he says this.

Celeste feels her eyes sting and fill again against her will.

Robin puts a hand on her shoulder. "People do get hurt; you're right. But that's no reason not to talk about it. There's no point in getting sanctimonious, better just to see it."

"I'm not talking about getting sanctimonious." Celeste's voice is stronger now. "I'm just trying to figure out how you're supposed to love someone. How are you supposed to be good if nothing is bad?"

"Your problem is vocabulary," her father says. "Good and bad aren't particularly helpful words."

Harry told them where to go, and when they reach the parking lot at the trailhead, it becomes apparent that this is not going to be an easy hike. The trail up the mountain is more like an avalanche of rocks.

Celeste climbs ahead, watching her own strong thighs. The others stay together, talking. Occasionally, Celeste loosens a rock with her foot and sends it jumping down the trail behind her. "Rock," she yells, without turning around.

The day is hazy and thick with heat. Above her on the mountain, the tanned backs of college girls wearing bikini tops disappear around a bend. Sweat trickles from beneath her hair, and her breath is fast and heavy. When she stops and looks back, her father and his friends are gone, lost behind a turn in the path.

The trail ends abruptly two miles later at the edge of a cliff. The college girls are there, standing at the edge, taking pictures of themselves on the precipice of all that green oblivion below. "Will you?" they ask, holding out phones to Celeste as she arrives, gasping for breath.

She takes their phones and arranges the girls in the frame of each one. All those beautiful girls and behind them, all that space. She tries to get it just right, to capture the height and danger of their position. When she's done, she too sits at the edge, dangling her feet, feeling the pull of gravity at the soles of her shoes. She has one of those rare present moment feelings that makes her feel like a natural Buddhist at heart.

When her father and his friends arrive almost half-an-hour later, making a big show of how old and tired they are, Celeste is glad to see them. The college girls have gone back down the mountain, and it's just the four of them up there, eating handfuls of trail mix and speculating on what it would feel like to fall from such a height.

"Sometimes," Robin says, "I feel as if I have to stop myself from jumping. Not in a suicidal way, just because it could be so exuberant, you know?" They do know. They all nod. Celeste loves them again. She feels a surge of affection for these people she has known all her life—for her father's friends, these good people of Lake George.

When they get back to the house, Harry makes them all gin and tonics in big glasses. He's in fine spirits and Celeste suspects he's missed them.

"How did the Swiss Family Robinson do?" he asks.

Mariah flops into one of the wide wicker chairs and says, "Celeste is the only young one left."

"Not all that young anymore, either," says her father. "I can't believe I have a thirty-one-year-old daughter."

"Speaking of your daughter, the young doctor called. Isaac, is it?"

"It's *Ian*, Harry. Jesus!" Robin says, setting her glass down too firmly on the table. "You'd think you were jealous the way you go on about him. I suppose it's good we never had a daughter."

Celeste calls Ian from her room. "I miss you," she says, when voicemail picks up. "This place makes me feel like a teenager, and I'm tired of sleeping alone. Four more days."

When she hangs up, she stays on her stomach on the fold-out bed in the shrine room. Outside, the light is fading, and there's the sound of some insistent bug banging against the screen. The room smells of sandalwood incense and laundry detergent.

There's a knock at the door, and Celeste sits up quickly as if she has been doing something wrong. Harry opens the door.

"Oh." he says. "You're off."

"Voicemail."

"Well, I didn't want to disturb you. I'm making another round, just came to collect your glass."

Celeste looks to the nightstand where her half-full glass is sweating big clear drops down the side. "I'm good for now, but I'll come with you."

She gets up, grabs her glass, and puts her arm through Harry's. They walk arm and arm down the hallway, and Celeste wishes they could continue like that into the living room. What she wants is for everyone to know. She's tired of this complicated secret, and sometimes she feels sure that the truth of the matter would be good for them all. She imagines that Robin will not mind so very much, that she might, in fact, understand it perfectly. Seven years! Could it really have been so long? These people more than anyone else might understand her position, that she has never meant any harm, that she has been able to love them all this whole time.

Before they reach the threshold of the living room, Harry detaches his arm from hers, gives her bottom a light pat, and they enter the room separately.

"Found her in there just mooning away. Must be some guy, this young doctor," he says to the room in general, but only Mariah turns to smile at her. She's the only one susceptible to images of newlyweds mooning over each other.

Robin is busying herself with little dishes of nuts and olives. It's the time of day in which they all sit around eating cashews and drinking cocktails. A few drops of rain patter against the boards of the deck outside, and Celeste watches the tiny storm travel, like someone's personal bad day, out over the lake and then disappear as if it's been sucked back up into the cloud.

"I believe she used to moon for me like that," Harry says, as he twists the cap off the gin. "Of course, that was a long time ago. When she was just a girl and when I was…what was I? When I was the handsome older man. Still impressive."

Celeste turns away from him and feels her lips start to stretch into a tight false grin. The room is quiet except for the sound of Thelonious Monk playing softly. She doesn't have time to understand how the others are taking this.

"Harry," she says, "I never mooned over you." A dry, fake laugh like a cough comes from her throat.

"If you didn't," he continues, "It was only because I made myself too available to you."

Celeste hears the slop and fizz of tonic being poured over ice.

"Harry," Robin says, "What the fuck are you taking about? You're drunk."

"Yes," he says calmly, "I am."

"Poor Harry," Celeste's father says. "He loves to believe the young girls are mooning over him. I hate to break it to you, Harry, but your moonable days have come and gone, my friend."

Harry looks at her father. "I know that," he says impatiently. "I know she doesn't moon over me anymore. I'm talking about *before*. I'm talking about before everyone got so goddamned old."

They're all looking at him now, and no one has bothered to turn on the lights. It's dim. Soon they'll light candles, and Robin will put pasta on to boil. This should be their last cocktail before Harry goes to the cellar for wine.

"Even then," Celeste hears herself saying, "even then I didn't long for you. It's never been like that. Being with you was like being looked at. But I didn't look back at you, Harry, not like you hoped."

Harry is stirring the drinks, four of them in a row, gleaming and tinkling cheerfully.

"What the fuck are you talking about?" Robin is still sitting next to her father on the couch. She's looking at Celeste. Her hair is fanned prettily against her cheek.

"It's been such a long time now—since we were still in the house on Barn Road," Harry says. It was the house he and Robin rented for years before they bought their own place, and they can look out across the lake now and see it if they want. Celeste remembers her initial desire for Harry whenever she passes the house, remembers what it was like before there was a husband in San Francisco and before Harry seemed like a problem. What she remembers is the smell of lake water on their skin and the feeling that what was happening was somehow inevitable, natural, beautiful. She lowers herself into one of the wicker chairs facing the lake. "I don't want to do this anymore. I haven't for a while," she says.

Her father stands, suddenly, as if he might be about to lunge, but then he's left standing stupidly, looking old and unable to do anything, and he sits back down.

"My God," Robin says, regaining herself, "aren't we unconventional? A confession and a break-up right out in the open. Is there nothing we don't share?" She opens a drawer in the coffee table, takes out a pack of cigarettes and lights one. They're her "tipsy reserve" for moments of desperation.

"Celeste," her father says, making his voice low and ominous like he used to when she was misbehaving as a child. "What are you doing?"

"I'm trying," Celeste says softly, looking out at the hypnotic surface of the lake, "to be good. I'm trying to be a good person."

"There's no such thing as being good," Harry says, "only being human."

"Shut up, Harry!" Robin says, viciously, through clenched teeth.

"I'm trying to confess. But that's the wrong word because there is no one to absolve me." Celeste is taking deep breaths to keep her voice from shaking. The room is almost dark now, and they have all become dusky silhouettes. It's better that way. No one wants to look at anyone else.

"It wouldn't help," Harry says. "You're not that kind of person."

"What about Ian?" her father asks. He sounds confused, and Celeste suspects he's still trying to save the situation.

"I can't tell him. He doesn't know."

"I suppose *I* can take this, and he can't?" Robin asks.

"You know more about these things than he does. For him, things aren't complicated. He thinks good people don't do bad things."

"People are people. No good, no bad, just what is," her father says.

Celeste turns away from the lake, toward her father on the couch. "Jesus Christ with that Buddhist crap! There *are* bad things. We did a bad thing."

"I don't think he's saying you didn't. He's trying to tell you that you're not a bad person. He's absolving you, Celeste," Robin says. She's snuffing out her cigarette and lighting another. Someone has finally turned on a lamp in the living room, and the blue smoke swirls in its glow.

"I've always loved you both," Harry says. He's still standing at the kitchen counter behind his four gin and tonics. "Robin—" he starts, but then he looks down silently.

"For God's sake, give me my drink," Robin says.

Harry comes out from behind the kitchen counter holding the four drinks like a diner waitress. He passes them out to Mariah, Robin, and Celeste's father, who take them silently, without meeting Harry's eyes. Celeste remembers her own now-watery drink and picks it up. If someone were to look in on them, it would appear as if they were toasting. Simultaneously, they lift their glasses to their mouths and drink.

Robin says, "You should go back to your husband. This won't be the same now. You should just go back."

"I will. I'll leave tomorrow." Celeste looks at Harry, who's retreated behind the bar. "I'm sorry," she says, and she is.

The room is silent except for the music tinkling softly from the speakers near the ceiling. It's a beautiful night, and through the glass doors they can see the almost dark sky, the storm clouds are huge puffs of gray lined in the violet of bruises.

"I suppose we should all get terrifically drunk," her father says.

"Someone's got to make dinner," Robin says, heaving herself off the couch. "I'll put water on for pasta if Harry will start mincing garlic." She goes into the kitchen, and Harry hands her one of the huge pots hanging from the rack above their heads. She fills it with water, puts it on the stovetop, and turns back toward them. "The worst thing is," she says, her eyes brimming, "I loved these weeks. I really did."

WALKING WOUNDED

Here's something I learned only recently: If you're of a certain age and are having what your gyno calls a "welcome back" period after a year of thinking all that business was over, you might, because of a myriad of factors, including a brain that skips and stutters like a corrupted hard drive, possibly lose track of a tampon. And if that happens, do not, under any circumstances, squat over a hand mirror with a flashlight. It's the wrong impulse. If you lose track of a tampon, it's best to go straight to the professionals.

Recently, my fifteen-year-old daughter has been worrying about Alzheimer's, her own. My grandmother, her great-grandmother, suffered from the disease, and I think perhaps, even though my grandmother died nearly twenty years before Ellen was born, the nature of genetics has started to sink in. I spent many years worrying about Alzheimer's, my own. And then, I stopped. I'm not sure why. Some combination of faith in science, antidepressants, and the realization that worrying wasn't doing anything to protect me from these terrible ghosts. Plus, my worrying kept my husband up at night. "I can hear you buzzing," he would say, putting the pillow over his head.

But lately, I wonder. It's not that I left my car running in my driveway overnight or that I failed to turn off the burner after cooking my morning eggs. It's not that I couldn't remember Paul Rudd's name for the life of me, or the fact that I forget doctor's appointments and hair appointments and therapy appointments and DMV appointments. Okay, it's partly those things. It is definitely those things. But it's the tampon that really brings it all home.

A rewind. My beautiful, kind, smart, funny, athletic, thoughtful, artistic fifteen-year-old daughter Ellen is in treatment for an eating disorder. Of all the worries I've entertained through parenthood—from car accidents to kidnappings—I somehow managed to skip this one. My kids were much too well-adjusted and grounded to suffer from such a trendy illness. I'm a feminist. Ellen is a feminist. An eating disorder wasn't on the menu. So I failed to read the signs even when she started fainting during soccer games and looking both pale and gray. Even when I could see her long legs getting skinnier and skinnier.

What being in treatment for an eating disorder means, among other things, is that George and I must once again prepare, plate, and monitor every single meal and three snacks a day while Ellen sulks and cries the same big fat tears she cried as a toddler and tells us she'd rather die than eat a chicken thigh. We fight bitterly over a bowl of mac and cheese and some roasted broccoli. It means soothing her later when she comes back to us, filled with remorse. Last night she said, "I don't hate you; I hate eating." It means letting her sleep with one of us each night because she doesn't "trust herself." When we ask what she thinks she might do if left alone, she shrugs and cries. Even her fingers look skinny to me now.

All this is to explain why I brought my daughter with me to the ER to get my missing tampon removed. Yes, I tried the gyno's office like a normal person; they informed me that the tampon must absolutely come out *immediately* and that they couldn't possibly squeeze me in that day. Off to the ER, then. I thought it would be an in-and-out situation. Afterward, we'd go to the fancy art supply store for acrylic brushes, maybe stop for bubble tea, which is something Ellen will ingest.

But I had somehow forgotten about COVID. So, of course, she couldn't wait in the waiting room with me. She would have to wait in the car. And although I felt bad for her, I didn't have the bandwidth to think about it, because I was drowning in humiliation. I was fifty years old, and at the ER because I had lost a tampon. In my vagina. I apologized to everyone I encountered: The guy monitoring the check-in line, the intake nurse, a random EMT who had no idea what I was talking about. Then I went to the waiting room and tried to read a book about a Somali nomad.

After an hour, I called George and asked him to pick up Ellen. It was time for her noon feeding. He could make her eat and then take her to the fancy art supply store. (We're currently indulging all creative and expressive impulses, from painting to cartilage piercing.)

When I was finally led into the exam room, I apologized to the nurse and requested a female doctor. Minutes later, an exceedingly handsome male doctor arrived, ready to explore. I apologized again and then the doctor said the kindest thing. "Don't worry about it. It happens all the time. And, trust me, tampons are the least of what people lose inside their bodies."

I loved him for being funny and cavalier and not cringing or wincing even once while he stuck various things into my vagina—a giant cotton swab, a speculum, an ultrasound wand, his hand. After much searching, the handsome doctor couldn't see it, but he thought he could feel it. He would have to call a gynecologist down to confirm.

Left alone in the room while they paged the gynecologist, I had lots of time to retrace my steps from the day before, the day I started using tampons again for the first time in a decade. And not just any tampons, tiny little teenage tampons I stole from Ellen's backpack.

I began to wonder if perhaps I was mistaken. The only thing more humiliating than going to the ER for a lost tampon is going to the ER for a phantom lost tampon. I was on hour three of my ER journey and now fervently hoping someone would find an errant tampon inside my body. The alternative seemed infinitely worse.

Here's a secret: before we realized that our daughter was starving herself, I sometimes felt a quiet gladness about her slim long leggedness. If there was nothing to be done about my own body, at least I had produced this willowy girl. I had, as my mother had always advised, "bred the short legs out of the line." I was even weirdly impressed when my daughter got down to movie star wispiness at the beginning of her freshman year of high school, a blurry COVID year she spent attending class from her unmade bed and drinking ice water to stave off hunger.

I now spend my days reassuring her. She will get better. She is not losing her mind. She does not have to be a perfect student. She does not need to scold or punish or compare herself. I pet her hair, her forearms, her legs. I hug her constantly. The way I love her is a source of wonder to me, painful and delightful, both. But I'm only pretending to be better at this than she is. At night I'm still twenty years old, wishing I could slice away my own unwanted flesh like prosciutto.

The gyno arrived wearing a pride flag pin and silent, squishy clogs. She didn't use a speculum; she didn't need one. She knew vaginas like the palm of her hand and after feeling around with her gloved fingers, she declared my vagina empty. "It's not like it goes on forever. It's a finite space," she told me when I asked if she was absolutely sure. I apologized. She assured me it was no big deal. But I have a friend who's an ER doctor, and I know for a fact that they roll their eyes at the weird ones, the crazy ones, the ones who needlessly take up their time. I knew for a fact that someone would roll their eyes about me later. I used all the accumulated strength of my adulthood not to care.

The trip back through the reception and check-in desk was another walk of shame. I hunched my shoulders, made myself as small and unnoticeable as I could. When I got back to my car parked on the barren street behind the ER, I realized my keys were locked inside. I could see them in the cupholder. Of course they were. I gave the keys to Ellen so she could wait in the car. When George picked her up, she left them there. I called and he headed back to save me. It was so windy and cold outside I went into Petco to wait. Luckily, we actually did need cat food.

A week later Ellen hits herself repeatedly with the stick end of a cat toy causing dark, florid bruises to appear on her legs. It's the worst thing I've ever seen, and I'm again shocked. How can this be? How did we get here? Her impulse to hurt herself is a mystery to me.

I don't cry. Instead, I let the laundry pile up, order stuff off the internet, buy expensive gummies that hurt my teeth. I cancel plans, forget more appointments. At the newspaper where I work, I forget an entire week of the month exists and fail to schedule any stories for it. I don't leave the house. I buy more stuff off the internet. I plan and make meals. I sit and make my daughter eat eggs or pasta or brussels sprouts. I continue to bleed.

Later, she scratches the insides of her forearms until she bleeds. She looks like a junkie. It's unfathomable. I can't bear it.

Soon, we have four therapists, two psychiatrists, a nutrition-ist, a pediatrician, a gynecologist, and a general practitioner trying to make us better. It's not enough. Soon, our daughter might be hospitalized.

I think back to the isolation of early COVID with a kind of nostalgia. We picnicked on a golf course. We went to see empty tourist attractions in our own city: Coit Tower, the crookedest street in the world, a massive city park with views of the bay and the dump. We took long urban hikes past shuttered businesses. It was weird, but it wasn't that bad.

Or maybe it was, and I just can't remember it. Maybe then I was like an eager soldier at the beginning of a noble campaign, with hope and energy outweighing my dread. Now I am that same soldier, bedraggled, jaded: I know what this war is like.

Ellen goes back to in-person school this week for the first time in eighteen months. California is on fire, the sky becoming that now familiar yellow. A peach-colored light shines through the windows, eerily beautiful. Our friends have been evacuated from their home in the burning foothills. There are so many things to worry about.

We've just been to the doctor. Ellen has two new cuts on her inner arm and she's lost two more pounds. There's a demon inside her, a possession. I ask her whether she would starve herself to death if I stopped trying to make her eat. She shrugs. "Probably." I want to scream at her, shake her. I want to slap her. What is this disease? How did it get into her? And why couldn't it be weed, or booze, or teenage pregnancy? Why couldn't it be COVID?

I cry so hard on the way home from the doctor's I fear I might crash the car. This is the first time I've cracked in front of her. There is a demon inside me, howling. I can't help myself. When we get home, I rush to my room and scream into my pillows. I beat them. I pray. I thrash myself to sleep. When I wake up an hour later, Ellen agrees to eat a nectarine and twenty pecans, and I think, okay, maybe.

I can only do what I can do. Buy a box of my own tampons. Watch the time-lapse videos Ellen sends me of her eating lunch in the attendance office. Wake up early to make big breakfasts. I can bump my way through this new world, these weird days. But I'm confused, my internal compass is off. I've lost my focus and I forget so many things. I don't have Alzheimer's. But I do have something. I have everything. It's all so fucking awful because it's all so fucking beautiful.

A VERY GOOD GIRL

It all started with a bit of spit she almost couldn't muster. Dry mouth was another mild but irritating gift of middle age.

That was a year ago. The test had come back within a month and was unremarkable. The most interesting thing about her ethnic background, which leaned heavily Northern European, was the 17% Greek blood she carried in her DNA. Zero idea where that came from, but she appreciated it. The Greeks were impressive.

Now, because of that mail-in test she did out of boredom as much as curiosity, she and Beatrice were about to fly 2,000 miles to meet her half-sister, a woman named Elise, who lived in Evanston, IL, outside Chicago and bred Great Danes with her wife, Shayna. She had a sister. Bea and Eleanor had an aunt. That was infinitely more exciting than being 17% Greek.

It took a little time. There was the initial email, the disbelief, the tentative decision to respond, the cautious elation. That all happened before she even mentioned it to Bea, who was busy applying to colleges and not in the habit of having long conversations about her mother's life, or Eleanor, who was in Spain studying something about food and history that involved visiting fish canneries. Then there was the first awkward phone call.

Elise had a rich, confident voice. "I bet we have weird things in common. Like, what's your favorite food?"

The question stymied Kate. It all depended on her mood, the time of day, her location. "Donuts," she said because it was the first thing that came to mind. She liked donuts, but they were hardly a staple in her culinary life.

"Okay, so not that," Elise said. "I'm a prime rib lady, myself. The whole ball of wax—creamed spinach, popovers. That's my death row meal."

Kate poured herself a glass of Burgundy from the bottle sitting on the counter. It had been open for three days and was about to go vinegary. She wanted to amend her answer. Prime rib sounded delicious. But it was too late. She went into the living room and sat on the battered old couch. She and Vince bought it when Bea started kindergarten and they thought the messy years were behind them. That made it, God, thirteen years old. Too old for what was a cheap piece of furniture to begin with.

"Did you have braces?" Elise asked. "I wore headgear for an entire year."

Kate hadn't. But she had spent her adolescence hating the incisor that turned inward slightly on the right side and overlapped her front tooth. She'd since grown fond of it. "I probably needed them," she said to Elise, "But they were out of reach for my mom."

On their second conversation, Kate ended up telling Elise about Vince and the divorce. In her defense, Elise asked.

"It was mutual," she said, which was a fib. It was mutual because Vince wanted out and made her miserable until she wanted out too. "We're both better off. I got the house. He got to move to Hawaii. But it's sad for the kids. It's always sad for the kids."

"I always wanted my parents to break up. They were miserable," Elise said. Kate could hear ice clinking in her glass.

"You know, I think of our father as a real asshole. That's his legacy around here," Kate said, in case Elise misunderstood the situation.

"He was," Elise said. "In a lot of ways."

On their third call, Elise invited Kate and Bea to visit her and Shayna in Illinois. "If we get lucky, we might have a new litter in the house, which is always a good time."

Kate looked forward to meeting Elise with a giddy anticipation she hadn't felt since high school. She always suspected that the best thing in the world would be to have a sister. As the trip approached, she was tempted to buy new outfits and color her hair. She made an appointment to have her legs waxed and her eyebrows tinted. She hadn't done this much grooming since right before her wedding.

Kate told both her girls at the same time, during a Zoom call with Eleanor in Andalucía.

"I'm glad we're all here," she said into the laptop screen she and Bea shared. "I have some news."

"Can you stop yelling in my ear?" Bea said. The sting of Bea's curtness threw Kate off momentarily.

"Anyway," she started again, scowling at Bea. "Remember the DNA test I took?"

"Obviously, Mom," Eleanor said. "You started Duolingo-ing Greek."

"That was for maybe two weeks," Kate said. "Anyway, I guess people can find you in these DNA databases, and this woman found me, and it turns out she's my half-sister. Older. Her name is Elise. She's a lesbian."

"Of course Mom has to mention she's gay," Bea said to her sister.

"Did you hear what I said? I have a sibling."

"Wait," Eleanor said. She was drinking red wine like she was some sort of grown woman. "You have a sister? Whose? How is that even possible?"

"We have the same father."

"So, do we have cousins?" Bea asked.

"I told you, she's a lesbian."

"Oh my god, Mom, gay people have children all the time."

Their conversations were always veering off in a direction that made Kate feel desperately misunderstood. She took a deep breath. "I know gay people have children, but these particular ones do not. They have dogs, apparently."

"You hate dogs."

"I don't hate dogs," Kate said. "I just don't really understand them. Or why people like them so much."

Now it was the day they were leaving. More accurately, the day Kate was forcing Bea to join her on this trip to Illinois to meet their sudden relative.

"It's going to be so awkward," Bea protested as Kate struggled to get the warped front door closed properly. It was now well and truly beyond just needing a coat of paint, and she would have to replace it before she and Bea got stuck outside one day. Or inside. She wasn't sure which would be worse.

"It might. It might not. Maybe it'll feel like family right away."

"Doubtful," Bea said. Everything she was wearing was torn and gray and secondhand. Kate had to constantly resist the urge to comment on Bea's teenage runaway fashion sense.

"You can play with the puppies," Kate offered, which had more of a soothing effect on her daughter than she thought it would. It was easy to forget that seventeen-year-olds were still just children.

The plane from Denver to Chicago took two-and-a-half hours and Bea ignored Kate almost the entire time. Even through the grind of the airplane's engine, Kate could hear Megan Thee Stallion coming from Bea's headphones. Kate sat without getting up even once to use the bathroom and worked on crossword puzzles on her phone. She read constantly, but she wasn't very good at crosswords and not above googling certain answers. But there was no Wi-Fi on the plane, so she was doing even worse than usual. Still, it kept her mind occupied. If she stopped to look out the window, her jitters made her feel ill, so she stayed focused. "Greek fire," was a clue, and she confidently typed PYROS. Duolingo paid off.

In the rental car on the way to Evanston, Bea removed her headphones and said, "So I don't really get it. How is this person your sister?"

Kate explained it as well as she could, again. She, Kate, was the secret kid, and her mother the secret wife. This made Elise the real kid and her mother the real wife. Kate had only known her father until she was about seven, and then he'd disappeared and her mother married four men in fifteen years and then died single in a one-bedroom apartment on the carriage road off Hwy. 36.

"That's fucked up," Bea said, stretching her legs out on the dash. "That he just stopped seeing you. I fucking hate men."

"They're not all bad."

"But aren't you, like, mad? I mean, at least Dad, like, calls us and takes us on vacation and stuff."

"Mad never really came into it. But I've often felt quite sorry for myself."

Bea laughed. Kate loved it when she could make her daughters laugh. "But, like, she got a dad, and you didn't."

"At the moment I'm more, I don't know…. Honestly, I'm kind of embarrassed. I feel like I'm imposing."

"She invited us."

"Not on her home. Maybe on her family? I'm the bombshell here. I always knew I had a fucked-up family. I think Elise was under the impression she was normal until I turned up."

It took forever to get to Evanston, and it was nearly six when they found the house, brick with black trim and baskets of winter-withered geraniums hanging from the porch. The lights shone yellow through the leaded glass in the front door.

"Leave your bag," Kate said. "I hate showing up with luggage."

"Don't be so nervous," Bea said, her raggedy backpack hanging off one shoulder as always.

"Don't tell me how to be."

When she was in college, Kate had a pair of glasses that gave her an alter ego. They were black and aggressively large, and with them on, she became Inez, the feminist film critic. Inez was smart and stylish and tolerated zero shit. She was someone Kate could reference long after the glasses were gone. Inez didn't suffer fools, and she was a helpful guide, especially for situations involving fucked-up men.

The woman who answered the door was Inez at sixty. Her long graying braids were coiled into a loose twist and held to her head by a big tortoiseshell claw. She wore a burgundy kaftan and had silver bangles up one arm. Her glasses were thick and stylish. Kate felt herself looking like a Denver housewife and regretted her cropped jeans and Target sneakers. She should have at least worn black.

"I'm Shayna," the woman said, opening the door wider and motioning them in. "Elise," she called into the house. "They're here."

The house was low and dark and smelled of something spicy on the stove. The first thing Kate noticed when Elise came in, wiping her hands on a dishtowel, was that they didn't look alike. Elise was a former blonde whose cropped silver hair was stylishly mussed. She had one of those naturally lean bodies Kate always associated with the Dutch. Kate was shorter and rounded with big boobs and a thick mane of brown hair that thwarted all efforts to look "put together." Her unruly hair was one of the main reasons Kate never would have made it in the corporate world. Maybe her smile was recognizable? Elise had a huge, thin-lipped smile that maybe reminded Kate of herself.

"It's you," Elise said, hugging Kate and then backing away, her hands still on her shoulders to get a better look. "It's my sister. Can you believe it?"

Kate couldn't. Having a sister felt magical, as if a fairy Godmother had suddenly appeared and granted her childhood wish. She stared, probably mouth-breathing. Shayna's bangles jingled. Bea stood near the door, most likely dying of embarrassment. Kate was manifesting her worst, most awkward self.

"Hi!" Kate said at last, trying to sound peppy, normal, something other than dumbstruck. "Do we look alike?"

Shayna stood back, a red-nailed finger on her lip. "Maybe in the mouth," she said, examining them together.

Elise let go of Kate and moved to Bea. "My niece! I love your sneakers."

Bea looked down at her battered purple Converses. "Thanks."

After they collected their bags from the rental car and were shown to their room—a real guest room with matching twin beds and jaguar wallpaper—they went to meet Harriet, the pregnant Great Dane who was panting on her enormous bed in Shayna's and Elise's room.

"She's ready to pop," Elise said, getting down on the floor to pet her. "Sometimes we can see the puppies squirming around like aliens through her skin. Hopefully, they'll come while you're here." The dog was impressive with a shining gray coat and a head like a horse. She looked up at Kate and Bea with giant, watery eyes, but her attention was elsewhere.

"Is she in labor?" Kate asked. The air in the room was overly warm and smelled like dog.

"She's certainly getting ready. It's her second litter, so she knows what she's doing."

"That's cool," Kate said. She considered bending down to stroke Harriet's giant ears but refrained.

"She's a very good girl," Shayna agreed.

Elise invited them into the kitchen so they could chat while she finished the tagine. "I can offer you juice, sparkling water, or tea. We're a sober household."

Kate had never wanted a glass of wine more in her life. She needed something to loosen her wooden tongue. "I'd love a sparkling water," she said. Bea chose cranberry juice, which Kate had never before seen her drink.

"It's so interesting that we're both only children," Elise said. She was chopping bunches of herbs with the precision of a professional chef. "Then again, it was probably pretty expensive to keep up two households. Dad couldn't afford more of us." She laughed.

Dad. She said it as if they had been spending Christmases together their whole lives, as if there existed a man they collectively referred to as Dad.

"He didn't really keep up our household once he left."

"That must have been hard. How old were you again?"

"Seven."

There was a slight pause while Elise fussed about the stove. Kate noticed the music for the first time, something hip and clubby playing softly in the background.

"So, are you Greek? My DNA thing came out with a lot of Greek," Kate asked. This was her first real attempt at conversation aside from complimenting the house.

"So did mine! I was weirdly excited about it. I had no idea."

"He must have been Greek then. Or part Greek."

"I guess he was. He grew up in an orphanage, you know. I doubt he had any idea."

Kate didn't know about the orphanage. She knew almost

nothing, but she pictured her long lost Greek relatives as mourning old ladies dressed in black lace.

"I wonder if there are more of us out there," Elise said. "I mean, if he had one secret family. Maybe we have a whole group of siblings."

A whole group of siblings had been Kate's most lasting childhood fantasy. Instead, she got three teenage stepsisters from her mother's third husband, all of whom showed zero interest in her existence and then disappeared from her life as quickly as they had come. Laura, Lynn, and Lanette were their names.

"I'm not sure I could handle that," Kate said. "One surprise sister is a lot."

"Well, I, for one, am thrilled," Elsie said, taking the steaming tagine off the stove and asking Bea to bring the salad to the table.

Kate wanted to say that she too was thrilled, but her timing felt off. Instead, she said. "I'm just going to wash my hands." She went back upstairs to avoid using the powder room off the kitchen. She needed a breath. For one thing, she didn't know if she liked tagine. For another, she seemed to have forgotten how to make conversation.

She was drying her hands when there was a soft knock at the door. "Mom, it's me."

Kate opened the door for Bea.

"I'm getting high," Bea said, brushing by Kate and closing the door behind her.

"What?"

"I'm having one small toke because this is hella weird. You probably should too. You're like this nervous little mouse."

Until this moment, Kate wasn't sure Bea had ever tried pot. "You can't smoke in here!" Kate whispered. "They'll smell it. They're sober for chrissake."

"It's a vape. It doesn't even smell. Besides, we can blow it into the fan. That's what I do at home." Bea sucked on the end of the contraption balled in her fist and blew a long stream of smoke, or steam, or whatever it was, into the grate of the fan whirring on the ceiling. Then she handed it to Kate.

"We're discussing this later," Kate said.

Bea showed her how to use the vape and Kate sucked a large, painless lung full and then blew the smoke into the fan. She rinsed her mouth out with tap water and the two of them headed back downstairs. "This better not mess me up," Kate whispered, squeezing Bea's hand.

Kate liked tagine, as it turned out. And she liked the salad, and the warm, pillowy pita bread. In fact, she was having one of the best meals of her life.

"So," Elise asked, "you work in a bookstore. That sounds like an absolute dream job. We're both big readers." Kate had noticed their packed bookshelves in the living room.

She chewed and swallowed. Her mouth was unbelievably cottony, and she gulped water. "I own the bookstore, co-own it, so it's not, you know, all that romantic. I worry about things like cost per square foot and whether we have the lowest rates on our credit card processing service."

"I pictured you reading all day with your feet up while quiet, reverent customers came in to browse contentedly."

"Yeah, I always feel like I'm letting people down when I tell them the truth. Everyone *thinks* they want to own a bookstore, but it's still a business, you know?" Kate helped herself to more tagine. "This is incredible, by the way."

Elise asked Bea about the colleges she had applied to and Bea gave her a minimalist answer. Bea's approach to the whole process had been to stay as detached as possible. Maybe she wouldn't even go to college in the fall. What a waste that would be. Vince's parents had offered to pay.

"And what about your sister? Do you two get along?" Elise asked.

To Kate, Bea looked incredibly stoned. Her eyes were heavy-lidded and red. Did vaping with her daughter make her a bad mother? Pot was legal in Colorado and Bea would be eighteen in four months. That had to count for something. And yet, it felt much worse than when she let Bea and Eleanor drink beer on a camping trip last summer. Her own heart was starting to thump uncomfortably, and her skin felt greasy, as if something were oozing out of it.

"We text a lot," she heard Bea say.

"And they don't include me," Kate said, sticking her lower lip out impetuously and then immediately feeling ridiculous. "I'm kidding! I'm kidding!"

Bea gave her a side eye and Kate helped herself to more salad.

"Are you ok?" Shayna asked, looking at Kate.

She tried to take a deep breath but couldn't fill her lungs. "I'm fine."

"You look a little unsteady."

Kate smiled and felt heat prickle up from her chest to her hairline. She grabbed her water glass, but it was empty. Her cheeks sizzled. "I'm just a little flushed."

"I'll get you some more water." Shayna stood with Kate's glass and went into the kitchen.

"Mom!" Bea said under her breath. "Keep it together."

But Kate was having a very hard time keeping it together. She couldn't get a proper breath and all that idiotic stuff she had said about the bookstore was getting braided together in her mind. Had she been rude? Did Elise think she was rude?

Shayna returned with her water and Kate tried to look normal taking the glass, but her face was on fire and she was speaking so slowly. She drank and looked up. They were all looking at her with worried little creases in their foreheads.

"All good. All good," she said, but her voice was somehow squeaky and lumbering at the same time.

"Hot flash?" Elise asked.

"Yeah, maybe," Kate said. Underneath the table she squeezed her own leg to make sure she wasn't dreaming and to confirm that she was actually fucking up meeting her sister in real life. She was. She was actually fucking it up. In real life. She was going to kill Bea.

She could hear them talking among themselves, but it felt as if they were on another level somewhere above her.

"I'm not really into sports," Bea said in response to something. Kate looked at her and saw only how enormous her pores looked, how messy her hair was.

"I'm good," Kate said.

"Mom! No one said anything."

"Oh, sorry. I just. I'm not sure what's wrong with me. I feel very strange."

"It's a strange situation for sure," Elise said.

"Do you want to talk about our dad now?" Kate asked. She sat up straight, trying to appear normal.

"Are you high?" Shayna asked.

Kate's mouth was once again terribly dry. She stifled a laugh that had bubbled into her throat.

"Are you?" Shayna asked, looking at Bea.

"No!" Bea said.

"Because you know you can't do that here."

"I'm so sorry," Kate said. "I didn't mean to." There was a hiccup near her sternum that wouldn't rise.

"You're high? Wait. Really?" Elise said. "Why would you be high?"

"You should probably leave," Shayna said. "This is a sober household."

"No, please. I want to meet my sister. I don't even smoke pot." Kate finished her glass of water and let out a low moan.

"I can't believe how disrespectful this is," Shayna said.

"Now, wait. Just wait. What happened?" Elise was folding and unfolding her Indian print napkin into little pleats.

"I think I have to lie down." Kate felt her stomach's contents in her throat. Her cheeks still flamed, and her whole body felt parched and overheated. She was afraid she might throw up. She picked up her empty water glass and dry heaved into it. There was a collective wince at the table. "Can I please go lie down?"

Shayna stood up. "Go pull yourself together."

"I'll bring you a glass of water," Elise said, getting up from the table. "Sleep it off."

Kate spent what felt like an eternity lying on her back in the well-decorated guest room, her body throbbing with humiliation. When Bea came in to check on her, she hissed, "What in the world was in that?"

"It was just weed, Mom. God. I can't believe you're such a lightweight."

"How are you not freaking out?"

"I'm just more used to it."

Kate closed her eyes. She had four more months as her daughter's keeper. There was so much advice she forgot to give, so many things she hadn't taught her. Like, did Bea know you were supposed to tip hotel maids? Could she check her tire pressure? Did she even know when tomato season was? Kate could feel her breath getting shallow again and she tried to suck in air and expand her ribcage, but it was creaky and brittle. Her lungs wouldn't fill.

"Do you know your social security number by heart?"

"What?" Bea asked.

"Never mind. We'll talk about it later."

She closed her eyes and her mind unrolled like a filmstrip. She couldn't slow it down to hang on to a thought. I wonder who our dad liked better, she thought as she drifted to sleep. And then she laughed. The answer was so obvious.

It was pitch dark when she awoke, and she was still in all her clothes. Her eyes and mouth burned and puckered. She was still stoned, but now her mind moved slowly instead of unspooling too quickly.

"Mom!" Bea called her softly from the doorway.

"What time is it?"

"Like eleven or something. The puppies are coming."

It took Kate a second to understand the sentence.

"Come see."

Kate sat up, feeling puffy and bloated, as if she had a pillow stuffed under her shirt. "The puppies?" she said back.

"Come watch. It's kind of gross, but it's cool."

"I don't think I can face them," Kate said. "I'm so embarrassed."

"I don't think they're that mad anymore. Everyone's excited about the puppies. One came out already."

"Trust me, they're that mad." Kate heaved her giant, bloated body off the bed. "I need to take a shower. I'm," she rubbed her face, "filmy."

"You really shouldn't smoke weed."

"Obviously, Bea."

"Come watch after you shower. We don't know how many are in there."

Kate showered, letting her burning face linger in the cool water. Her mind still felt slightly out of grasp.

Before she went into the bedroom to witness the births, she crept downstairs and drank a tumbler of cranberry juice, letting the tartness reawaken her salivary glands. That was a little better.

Shayna, Elise, and Bea were sitting cross-legged on the floor next to the dog's bed, which was as big as a twin mattress. The dog's abdomen heaved and tensed, but she was quiet. Already nuzzling a nipple was a tiny, slick puppy about the size of a shoe. Harriet licked her puppy and occasionally looked curiously toward her backside, where another shiny puppy head was halfway out. Bea was right. It was kind of gross.

"Good girl," Elise cooed. "What a good mama you are." The dog ignored her.

Shayna squatted like a catcher, ready to receive the puppy as it emerged.

From the doorway, Kate watched as Harriet's body rippled and a be-sacked puppy slid out in a gush of brownish liquid. She felt queasy. Aside from her own, which were all about controlling pain, she had never before witnessed a birth.

Shayna removed the membrane from the puppy while Harriet sniffed it. Elise snipped the cord. While the dog licked her puppy clean with a tongue larger than her offspring's body, Shayna, Elise, and Bea exchanged smiles. "Another female," Shayna said.

Both puppies, small and black and blind, squirmed grub-like toward Harriet's prominent nipples.

"Should I help it reach?" Bea asked.

"Sure."

Bea carefully picked up the newest puppy with two hands and set it down so its mouth rested on one of Harriet's pink nipples. The puppy nuzzled clumsily and then latched on, still shaky and sightless.

"You can have a seat if you want," Shayna said, not turning to look at Kate who was still in the doorway. "It might be a long night."

Kate had the urge to fall to her knees and beg for forgiveness. Her body vibrated with the need for absolution. Instead, she walked toward the small circle and sat on the floor next to Bea. "Good girl," she whispered to Harriet, whose enormous head was near her feet, resting between contractions on the big bed. The entire situation was befuddling. All she could do was mimic the behavior of people who understood.

In the morning, Kate went downstairs and found it empty. The house was quiet although it was already nine. She searched for coffee and put on a full pot. While it bubbled and hissed, she went back upstairs to find the others. She'd gone to bed first. Everyone else stayed up to see all the puppies born. Bea wasn't in bed with her when she got up.

She found them in Shayna's and Elise's room. The women were in bed, but Bea was stretched out on the floor next to Harriet and the puppies, asleep with a throw pillow beneath her head. Harriet lifted her head when Kate entered. Six tiny puppies squirmed against her belly, squeaking and mewling. The mess of the birth had been cleaned up and that deep earthy inside smell was gone.

"We didn't get to sleep until after four," Elise whispered from the bed.

"I didn't mean to wake you," Kate whispered back. "Go back to sleep."

"Can you take Harriet to pee and fill her bowl? She doesn't need a leash."

Kate was stymied by the puppies who she didn't want to disturb, but when she patted her leg, Harriet did the work for her, nosing the puppies away and unfurling her enormous body into the standing position. She followed Kate out of the room, the puppies mewling louder and more desperately behind her. As soon as the front door was open, she lumbered down the stairs and peed on the small patch of lawn between the street and the sidewalk.

"Shall we take the air?" Kate said when Harriet finished. They made their way down the block. Kate couldn't tell if the dog's gait was post-labor soreness or just the result of being so large and ungainly, but they both walked slowly. There were patches of ice on the sidewalk, and Kate realized quickly she was seriously under-dressed for Chicago in March. She was from Colorado; she should have known better.

They turned the corner. "We may as well go all the way around."

Harriet looked at her, brows furrowed, and stayed by her side, occasionally leaning into her legs. Halfway down the block, Harriet backed into a street tree and hunched. Kate knew that people picked up their dog's shit—it was one of the many reasons she was glad not to be a dog person—but she hadn't thought to bring an implement of any kind. She looked around furtively but could see no one. She'd have to leave the shit, a crime that felt as transgressive to her as burglary.

When Harriet was done, they trotted down the block, fleeing their atrocity, and turned the next corner. The houses were similar bungalows with front porches and newer pop-ups in the back. Like Elise and Shayna's. Nineteen-twenties, Kate guessed. Occasionally, a 70s ranch house interfered with the symmetry. It was a nice neighborhood with big trees just about to bud lining the streets and dormant lawns that would be emerald and perfect soon enough.

Kate crossed her arms across her chest. She could feel her cheeks and lips chapping in the wind and her eyes watered. Harriet leaned heavily against her thigh, keeping that one spot warm.

"You're a good girl," Kate said, stroking one giant, silky ear. Harriet ignored her. Three women in athleisure and earmuffs passed them on the sidewalk, their breaths visible as little white puffs. "Get your walk in now," one of them said over her shoulder.

By the time they returned home, the blue sky had gone gray. They entered the house, and Harriet went straight upstairs while Kate went into the kitchen for coffee and warmth.

Shayna, Elise, and Bea were sitting at the kitchen table over mugs of coffee. It still seemed impossible that Bea drank coffee. All the tired old truths held. It did go so fast.

"The puppies basically freaked out when Harriet left and we couldn't sleep," Bea said.

Kate rubbed her hands together. "We had a nice little walk. I think it's going to snow."

"We're supposed to get six inches, maybe more."

"Jesus. I hope we can get out tomorrow."

Shayna sighed. "Well, you certainly can't leave today. They're already canceling flights."

"We can go to a hotel," Kate offered.

"Don't be silly," Elise said. "We can just start over, okay? We already talked to Bea."

Kate looked at her daughter, who stared into her mug. "I threw away my cartridge."

"What does that even mean?" Kate asked. She still hadn't had coffee. Her cheeks were thawing.

"My weed cartridge. I threw it away. I still have my vape, but the cart's gone."

"Thank God," Kate said. Bea glared at her. "I just mean, that was awful for me. Completely awful."

"Sorry," Bea said so softly Kate almost couldn't hear.

"It's not your fault, honey. I should have known better." She turned to Elise. "I was so nervous. I thought it would help."

"Our dad was an alcoholic, you know."

Kate didn't. She shook her head.

"Maybe you didn't spend enough time with him to know, but he was pretty awful. And the apple doesn't fall far from the tree and all that. But I've been sober for twenty years."

Kate didn't know what to say. Her memory of her father was so fuzzy, so polluted by her mother's anger and her own bewilderment.

"You're lucky in a way," Elise said. "Obviously he wasn't much of a father."

Kate's scalp prickled. She had never considered herself lucky in the father department. Or the mother department for that matter.

"I mean, he wasn't a mean drunk or abusive or anything like that. He was just, I don't know, drunk every single night. Out of it."

"That must have been hard."

"It was all I knew." Elise said.

Kate finally poured herself a cup of coffee.

"I really am so happy to find you," Elise said. "Both of you." She reached out for Bea's hand and miraculously, Bea held it.

"Me too," Kate said, sitting down. "I'm happy to have a sister. You have no idea."

"Our fucked-up dad did something right in the end."

"Passing along his DNA really wasn't that hard. Do we give him credit?"

"Probably not."

"Let's check on the puppies," Shayna said. "They were so desperate when Harriet left."

Harriet was back in her bed with the six puppies nestled once again into her side. Her head rested on the lip of her bed. Her eyes were closed. Kate supposed there was something regal about a dog so large and calm. She had dignity, which, in Kate's limited experience, most dogs seriously lacked.

The women stood over her in a semicircle. "What do you do with the puppies?" Kate asked. She hadn't thought about it before, but no one could keep six Great Danes.

"They're mostly all sold. We have people as far away as California and Texas waiting for these guys. We'll keep a female."

"We never had dogs growing up," Kate said.

"You didn't?" Elise looked incredulous. "Our dad was an absolute fanatic. We always had Great Danes. Harriet is the great-great-granddaughter of one of his dogs. Maybe one more great. I've lost track."

"She's like family then."

"Absolutely. I started breeding where Dad left off, but she's the best one ever." Elise gazed lovingly at Harriet.

"So, he gave you another good thing. Dogs."

"Harriet plus a sister. We're all related."

Kate laughed. Being related to Harriet wouldn't be so bad. She really was a very good dog.

"If you want, you can have the last female. She's the only one that isn't spoken for."

"Mom!" Bea said. "Yes."

Kate looked at the six squirming puppies, half charcoal gray, half spotted with black. They didn't disgust her, which was something.

"Our house is so small."

"No it's not. Not since Eleanor left." Bea nudged Kate's shoulder.

"Great Danes are very mellow, easygoing dogs. Especially Harriet's offspring," Elise said.

"But you'll be gone soon too and then it will be just me and the dog."

"Exactly, Mom. She'll keep you company."

Kate was only going through the motions of protest and saying the things she thought people should probably say when considering getting a dog. It was like so much of mothering, which was often merely imitating what an imagined good mom would do—limit sugar, enforce bedtime, impose curfews—even when she didn't really care about those things that much. She would take the dog, despite all the reasons she could give not to. In her second act, as the women's magazines called it, she would be a dog person.

"If you take her, we can deliver her to you in Colorado in about ten weeks and have another visit."

"Eleanor will be home by then," Kate said.

"That's wonderful. It'll be a family reunion."

You couldn't have a reunion if you'd never had a union in the first place, but Kate didn't say so. It was beside the point.

"Which one's mine?"

Elise hugged Kate, quick and tight. Then she got down on her knees and Kate followed.

They scanned the puppies until Kate found her, spotted and no bigger than a guinea pig. She lifted her from the pile of warm fur. "She's the runt."

Kate held out her cupped hands and took the puppy, still loose with sleep and newness. She had the urge to hold her to her bare skin as she'd been taught to do with her own babies so long ago. Instead, she held her up close and breathed in her sweet puppy smell.

Then she held the puppy aloft, *Lion-King*-style. "You will be called Helen, daughter of Harriet."

Elise clapped her hands and grinned. "That's so Greek."

Bea rolled her eyes. "Jesus, Mom. You're such a drama queen."

ACKNOWLEDGEMENTS

For their guidance, intelligence, time, love, and friendship I want to thank the members of my longtime writing group: Connie Biewald, Laura Catherine Brown, and Brooks Whitney Phillips, sisters all.

Some of these stories have their beginnings in previous decades and for all their incredible help and insight and laughter way back when, I'm eternally thankful for Lisa Taggart, Kate Chynoweth, Chris Markus, and Steve McFeely. For her endless cheerleading and faith, I will always be grateful to Sarah Creighton Kirley, who has been there from the very beginning.

I have two places I'm lucky enough to return to again and again to write. One is Leffingwell House in Aurora, New York and for that gift I'm incredibly grateful to Brooks Whitney Philips and her aunt, Pleasant Rowland, whom I've never met, but who changed my life. The other is the Wellstone Center in the Redwoods in Soquel, California, run by the epically lovely Steve Kettmann and Sarah Ringler. Over the years they have shared their amazing home with hundreds of writers and there is true magic to be found there. Thank you to their whole family, including Coco, Anais, and Sally.

I received support during the writing of this book from The Sustainable Arts Foundation. Thank you to Caroline and Tony Grant for their thoughtful and generous support of artists raising children.

Thank you to Leland Cheuk for reading this manuscript, remembering it, reading it again, and then publishing it. You've literally made my dreams come true. And, thank you to indie bookstores everywhere for being beacons of light in a harsh world.

To my parents Wayne Schoech and Caroline Berry, thank you for everything, including the big, beautiful mess of life. And last, but not least, to Pete Mulvihill for being my person. My best guess was a good guess.

ABOUT THE AUTHOR

Samantha Schoech's writing has appeared in *The Sun, Seventeen, The Gettysburg Review, Glimmer Train, Travel & Leisure, the New York Times,* and many other publications. She's the co-editor of two humor anthologies, including the bestselling *The Bigger the Better, The Tighter the Sweater.*

She has an M.A. in Creative Writing from UC Davis and she's been awarded numerous residencies, a Sustainable Arts Foundation grant, and the Erma Bombeck & Anna Lefler Humorist-in-Residence Award. In 2019 she co-founded the Rowland Writers Retreat in Aurora, New York.

She's the founding director of Independent Bookstore Day, and a staff writer at NYT Wirecutter. She lives with her bookseller husband and their twins in San Francisco.

7.13BOOKS